Trust Only No One

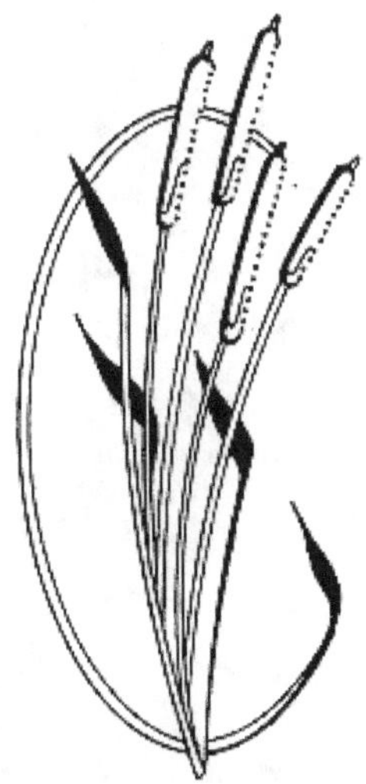

Trust Only No One

by D.C. Cole

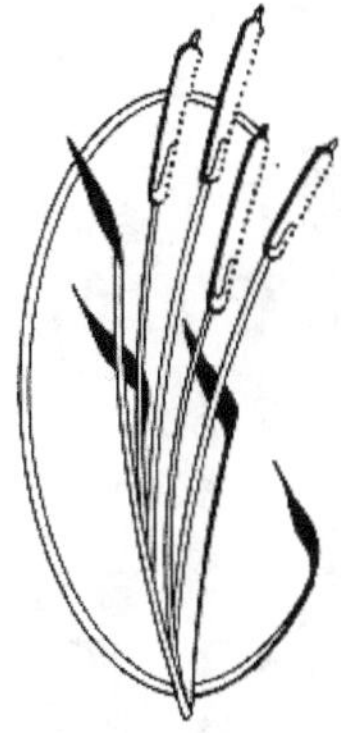

Editor
Cheryl Martin

Senior Publisher
Steven Lawrence Hill Sr.

Awarded Publishing House
ASA Publishing Company

A Publisher Trademark Title page

ASA Publishing Company
Awarded Best Publisher for Quality Books
105 E. Front St., Suite. 205, Monroe, Michigan 48161
www.asapublishingcompany.com

All Rights Reserved. No part of this publication may be reproduced, stored in a retrieval system or transmitted in any form or by any means electronic, mechanical, photocopying, recording or otherwise, without the prior written permission of the publisher. Author/writer rights to "Freedom of Speech" protected by and with the "1st Amendment" of the Constitution of the United States of America. This is a work of fiction. Any resemblance to actual events, locales, person living or deceased is entirely coincidental. Names, places, and characters are within the work of fiction and its entirety is from the imagination of its author.

Any and all vending sales and distribution not permitted without full book cover and this title page.

Copyrights©2011 D.C. Cole, All Rights Reserved
Book: Trust Only No One
Date Published: 08.2011
Edition: 1 *Trade Paperback*
Book ASAPCID: 2380559
ISBN: 978-1-886528-02-4
Library of Congress Cataloging-in-Publication Data

This book was published in the United States of America.
State of Michigan

A Publisher Trademark Title page

Trust Only No One

by D.C

I was waiting patiently in the corridor for my unpleasant husband Lord Dominic, who was as unpleasant as a cornered rattlesnake. He entered the corridor and yelled "Stand up and greet your husband, the lord of the manner in a proper way."

"Yes my lord," I said cowardly. "Dominic the cook has prepared a gourmet feast for your guests this evening. When shall they be arriving?" I asked cautiously, afraid that he may start ranting and raving.

"They will be here half past the hour, you should get yourself presentable so you don't embarrass me," Dominic ordered. "Oh and one more thing Lady Victoria?"

"Yes my lord," I said dreading his response.

"If I see Lord Stephan anywhere near you, I will have his head," Dominic demanded.

"Dominic I am not sure what you mean, there will be many guests here this evening, wouldn't it seem rude of me to ignore a guest?" I asked hoping he wouldn't get mad, but the look in his eyes told me he was furious with my questioning him.

Before I could step back I felt his hand across the side of my face. It knocked me backwards onto the seat.

"How dare you question me, I own you, and I say who you talk to and who you ignore, and if you choose to parade around like some floozy tonight, it won't just be Stephan's head I have, it will be yours as well. Do I make myself clear?" he screamed holding his hand up at me.

"Yes, my lord," I said cowering down to show submission.

"Good, now go get ready and get those brats ready as well, everyone knows they aren't mine, but they expect them to be well mannered and groomed well," he said holding his index finger up at me like I was incompetent or something.

"Sarah and Stephanie where are you?" I called when I entered their room, and they weren't there. "You know Lord Dominic has planned a very important dinner for this evening. There is supposed to be many important guests coming. There is even an ambassador or something coming so we must be on our best behavior. Otherwise Lord Dominic is going to be very unhappy, and we know how he is when he is unhappy," I told Stephanie and Sarah. The girls were my sister Violet's who had passed away when Stephanie was born, and their father was so grieved and stricken himself, he couldn't care for them, so I took them in and we raised them as ours. About a year or so after Violet's death, I heard the news of their father dying as well. Lord Dominic was not impressed with having to raise someone else's mistakes, as he would put it, but it made him look like a truly caring, and thoughtful man, so he agreed to raise them and give them all the benefits of his money and family.

While Sarah and Stephanie were picking out the perfect gown for this evening, I entered, and stated in shock, "you two look absolutely beautiful, but where are your gowns?" I had laid them out in the changing rooms, hanging on the door.

"Oh we're sorry, we didn't know, we'll rush and grab them."

"Oh no you don't I will go get them, I don't need you two prancing around in your slips, and upsetting Lord Dominic before his important gathering tonight," I told the two excited little girls. A short while later, I appeared with the gowns, "Here Sarah this one is for you," it was a pale blue with embroidered designs at the bottom, and was beautiful. "And this one is for you Stephanie," it was an adorable girlish pink color, with blue and purple flowers across the belt and bottom of it. "Now put these on and wait here until I come for you, we don't want any unpleasantness tonight".

"Dominic? The children are ready, is there anything you need me to do before I fetch the girls?" I asked, cautiously.

"Yes, check the kitchen and servants, make sure they are all set up and clean, I can't have any grungy servants running around," Dominic ordered.

"Yes my Lord," I said, as I went to check the kitchen and servants. As I entered the kitchen, I noticed the serving girl Lilly, had a little stain on her apron. "Oh no my dear, you must go and change your apron," before Lord Dominic sees.

"Yes my lady," Lilly said, and rushed out to change her apron. "Alright everyone, let me see, is there anything Lord Dominic won't approve of," I announced, as I scoped everything out. "Wonderful everyone, it all looks great, now if you don't mind, please bring the appetizers out to the social room, so when the guests arrive they can snack and talk."

"Yes Lady Victoria, as you wish," the cook Nigel said as he pointed to the trays for the servers to carry out.

"Sarah and Stephanie come here please?" I asked, as I walked to their room.

"Yes ma'am," Sarah answered.

"Oh my, you two look so wonderful. Now let's go over the rules for this evening. First; no fighting, or arguing with each other or anyone else, second; use your manners, and don't touch the appetizers or any other dish until it's offered to you, and third; which is just as important as the others, be ladies, and curtsy to any guest that you are introduced to. Also listen to Nicole, she is in charge of you this evening. Lord Dominic needs me to be at his side, and flatter our guests, and act as the Lady of the house."

"Yes ma'am, we will do as you ask, and obey." Sarah said. It was amazing how elegant and proper the children could sound, I thought to myself.

"Good, now come down stairs with me, and prepare to greet the guests."

"Yes ma'am" the girls chorused.

My gown glistened with elegance as I entered the social room. The gown was floor length, strapless, and wine colored with a matching wrap that draped gracefully over my shoulders. My hair was laying straight and lightly fell off my shoulders, with its reddish highlights shining through the ember colors as the light hit it. "Oh my goodness, Lady Victoria you look like you stepped right out of a fairy tale in that gown, I'm positive you are truly the most beautiful woman on earth," Nicole said in awe.

"Oh dear, you are too kind, thank you sweetie, you look stunning as well, my dear," I told Nicole.

"Where are the girls, madam?"

"Oh they will be right down," I answered.

"Oh they look just wonderful," Nicole exclaimed as she saw the girls coming down the stairs.

"Sarah, Stephanie you look absolutely delightful, I am so proud of you, you look just like little debutantes, now we must remember to act like it," I reminded them.

"We will," the girls announced proudly.

"Victoria, where the hell are you at? Why isn't my tie with my suit?" Lord Dominic bellowed.

"Oh no, Dominic is in a foul mood, right now I best go and see what I did," I said with fear dripping off every word.

"Dominic what is it, my lord?"

"My tie is not with my suit, and it's not my job to search for a damn tie. Hell, I am Lord of the manner and I will be damned if you all won't treat me like it."

"Oh my lord I will fetch it right now, and I am sorry. It is not your job to search for a tie, I mean you are the Lord of the manner and you will be treated like it. I will make sure from now on that things are exactly the way you want them," I said as I bowed at his feet

"Now that's more like it," Dominic said proudly as he puffed out his broad shoulders and chest as if he were a king, or a god even. "Now get going, the guests will be arriving any minute," he ordered.

Moments later, Luther, our butler entered and said, "Lady Victoria your guests are starting to arrive, is there something you would like me to tell them, as they wait?"

"No Luther, I will be out in a moment and greet them," I announced as I left the room and went to greet our guests. If there was one thing I knew how to do well, it was put on a fake smile and pretend everything was ok. I knew if things didn't go well tonight, it would take a hurricane to protect me from him tonight.

"Luther?" Lord Dominic called.

"Yes Lord Dominic, what can I do for you?" Luther asked.

"I need you to do me a favor. Watch Lady Victoria tonight, I want to know her every move, and who she talks to for more than three minutes. Lord Stephan will be here and I don't like how he looks at her, and she has always showed him more than just friendly hospitality. If she is talking or flaunting herself at him, I want to know," Dominic said.

"Yes my lord, anything you wish," Luther said, and

left the room. Luther knew how Dominic was, but he didn't dare betray him, because if he did, he would surely end up, jobless or worse, lifeless.

Dominic went to the social room where the guests would be, and began to mingle and boast about his latest victory. Many of the guests were very jealous of Dominic. He had more money than any of them and loved to brag about it. He had more power than any man should have, and he had a gorgeous wife, who was completely devoted to him, and would do anything for him, including obey his every wish. None of them had a clue of how I really felt about my husband. I despised Dominic, he was ruthless, mean, and controlling, but despite how I felt towards my husband, I made everyone think I loved him so much and valued him more than anything else.

"Lord Stephan, how do you do this evening?" I asked.

"Oh wow Lady Victoria, I swear you get more beautiful every day, how do you do it?" Lord Stephan flattered her.

"Oh you are too kind, and thank you, but I must go and see Lord Dominic. Later I will talk with you more," I said as I began to walk away. I hated to walk away from him, we had been friends since we were children, but I did not want to feel the wrath of Dominic tonight.

"Victoria there you are, I have been looking everywhere for you," Natasha said frantically.

"Hi dear, how are you?" I didn't see you come in, I said. "Is everything ok Natasha?

"No I have to warn you, I overheard Dominic telling a few gentleman that if he sees Lord Stephan even looking at you, that you will regret it beyond tomorrow, and Stephan will find himself a few feet underground," Natasha exclaimed!

"Oh no, please help me, don't let me even enter his eye site, can you do that Natasha?"

"Of course I can, someone needs to give Lord Dominic a taste of his own medicine, Victoria." Natasha blurted out.

"Now Natasha you know that won't happen, and bite your tongue, I have a feeling after the party I'm going to have a nightmare on my hands as it is."

Natasha and Victoria had been like sisters ever since they were young, and Natasha had always been the wild one. There is no man that could tame her, and no man would ever be her Lord. She inherited her family's estate and money when her great grandfather died. Funny thing, she went her whole childhood, living in an orphanage with me, and never knew her family had loads of money, until the day she turned 18. She received a letter from her grandfather who had passed away, just a few days prior. When Natasha opened the letter, and read it, she was stunned beyond words, how she had not known that she was wealthier than most of the men in the country. It is no secret to anyone of her wealth, and opinion on marriage, it is for rich men and poor women, and it's not for rich women and poor men. Natasha swore she would never marry and lose everything to any man. She may not have earned her money in the sense of working, but she spent her life in the orphanage, and that was her way of earning it, and she helps the orphanage every chance she can.

"Victoria you have got to do something before he kills you one of these days, or hurts the children," Natasha warned me, as if I wasn't worried enough.

"I know, but if I leave he will just hunt me down, and kill me anyway," I said with a sound of hopelessness in my voice. "Please Natasha lets go back to the party and enjoy the festivities, and make sure everyone thinks I have the perfect life."

"Ok let's go, besides I love making all these rich men feel beneath me," Natasha said with a giggle.

As we walked into the room, Natasha noticed Dominic watching Victoria like a hawk, and that made her nervous. Before she knew it Dominic was walking up to them with a wild look in his eyes. "Natasha you should go mingle, while I talk with him, please" I begged. "My lord, what can I do for you," I asked as he grabbed my arm so harshly, I thought it might snap right in half, but yet discreetly enough that only Natasha noticed, and became worried.

"Upstairs now," he ordered.

"Yes, my lord, what is it?" I asked quietly. Once out of the room, and half way up the stairs, where no one could see, he slapped me across the face.

"How could you do this, after all I've done for you, how could you?" he began to yell.

"What did I do, my Lord?" I said cowering down.

"You are off parading around with that whore of a friend, Natasha, and everyone knows how she is. I have men coming to me asking why I let my wife parade about doing whatever she likes," he continued to tell me as we reached the bedroom. "They all think you're just like her, and when you are falling all over Lord Stephan like some school girl, questions are being asked, and I will not tolerate it anymore," he said as he raised his hand to strike me again. This time the hit was hard and fierce, knocking me to the ground. The tears were streaming down my face.

"Now, I will send the girls up here to you, and I will explain to everyone that you are putting the children to bed, and that you decided to be a doting wife and mother to those brats, and stay up here with them," he said as he stormed out.

Wondering to myself, as I sat there on the edge of the bed, how I had become ok with this. This isn't a life, this is hell, everyday wondering when he will strike, what he will do, how I could have let myself believe this is a life, I wondered. I heard the girls crying, oh no panic seized me. Both girls were being dragged by their hair into the bedroom, by Dominic.

"What is it, My Lord, did something happen?" I asked. "Yes, I caught these two, laughing and running around like animals with some other children and look, they look like pigs," he said pointing to little stains on their dresses. "Here, you deal with these. I can't take much more of this, disobedience from you and these brats," he said. He raised his hand to strike them,

"No, Dominic" I yelled as I stepped in front of the children, and pushed them behind me, "you will not lay a hand on these girls, they did nothing wrong, it was my fault. I wasn't watching them. I was off parading around with Natasha, instead of doing my job. I am sorry, but if you need to strike someone, please strike me, for it was my wrong doing not theirs," I said as I bowed my head, and braced myself. I knew it was going to be fierce, because I stood up to him, and that was unacceptable in his eyes.

"Oh really," he said as he drew back, and with a very strange laugh, that sounded more like a mad man who had just been turned loose on an unsuspecting city, he swung so forcefully at me, I felt my cheek bone crack. The pain dropped me. I fell to the ground, and before I could move, I saw him strike both girls across the face. They fell to the ground, holding their cheeks, both so afraid to cry or anything, and he said with a smile, "you will not tell me who I can punish or who deserves to be punished, I am your god, and you will do right to remember that next time, because if I see you doing something I don't like, then I will punish the girls for it. That seems to get your attention," he said with a very loud gruff laugh, and walked out.

I tried to pick myself up, but it was too hard. My neck hurt so bad from the impact, how could a single man's hand be so powerful? I thought. I managed to crawl over to the girls, I needed to make sure they were alright.

"Girls, I am so sorry, are you ok?" I asked them as they were huddled together, with tears of fear streaming down their faces.

"Yes, we are ok, are you?" they asked, through sobs."

"Yes, I am ok, girls, but I need a moment to think," I told them.

"Lady Victoria, are you alright, what happened?" Nicole came rushing to my side. "Your face is swollen badly, you need a doctor."

"No", I said. "Please discreetly go and get Natasha, but let no one see you."

"Yes my lady, right away."

"Nicole, please be careful, no one must know, no one can see her come up here" I said.

"Of course, madam," she said and went to get Natasha.

A little while later, Natasha came in and with the "look" on her face. I had only seen that look on her face once before, and that was when we were kids. A boy pushed me in the mud, and hit me, and she let him have it. I knew I looked a mess, far worse than I did that day when we were kids, I couldn't imagine what was going through her mind.

"Oh my, what happened," she asked, as she rushed to me, and looked at my cheek.

"It doesn't matter, all that matters is that I get these girls out of here, can you help me?" I cried still very unsure of how I could do it. "I want to sneak out, while he is still at the party, I can't let him hurt these girls," I said as I stood up, and grew a back bone for the first time in my life.

"Of course, whatever you need, just tell me what I can do" Natasha said.

"Just get a few things, only vital ones for the girls, a few pairs of pants, shirts, and coats, that's all I need right now," I said.

"Right away," Natasha said. I began to take off my jewelry, and place it in the box; I knew I wouldn't need fancy things right now. I began to gather a few personal items, and put on a pair of jeans, and a t-shirt, with a sweatshirt over the top. Moments later, Natasha and the girls returned with pants and sweatshirts on, and Natasha had a bag in her hand of the girls' things.

"Now which way do you want to leave?" Natasha asked.

"I want you to go back to the party, like you never left, and after a while leave like normal. The girls and I will go out through the servants' quarters, no one will see. The servants are tending to the guests, and Nicole is coming with us," I said.

"Ok, I will do that but please be careful."

" Nicole, I hope you don't mind but I grabbed you a few of my clothes to put on after we leave, if you have anything important to you, you may grab it on our way out, but it must be quick," I told her.

"Yes, madam, but you and the girls are what are important to me, let's get a move on" Nicole said with a smile of relief. "I will carry Stephanie, and you carry Sarah, she is lighter," she said.

"Thank you, my dear," I said, as we scooped up the children and started to leave.

The Escape Chapter

The girls were very quiet, and barely moved while we walked out through the servants exit. I think they were scared but happy to be leaving, I thought to myself. Once outside we took the woods line, we knew no one but wildlife would see us.

It seemed like hours as we walked to Natasha's house to wait for her, but it had only been about an hour, and we would soon be there. "Just passed this brush we will be there," I said to them, and moments later we saw her house. Well castle is more like it. "Head lights," I said as I paused for moment in panic, hoping it wasn't Dominic coming to take us back. I saw with relief that it was Natasha, perfect timing I thought. We rushed to the car, where Natasha was waiting.

"Did anyone see you, or wonder why you were leaving?" I asked.

"No, I played it out perfect. No one knows a thing, and Dominic thinks you are all upstairs in bed, waiting for him. He's so stuck on himself to think you would actually leave him," Natasha said.

"Good, but we can't stay here, he will look for us here," I said.

"I know. I have the perfect place for you guys. I bought it a few years ago, planning for this day," Natasha said. "No one knows I have it or where it is, you will be safe there, but it is a drive to get there, so let's gets going," Natasha said.

"Ok, let's go girls," I said, as we got into the car to leave this nightmare.

Natasha was right, it was a drive. We had been driving for hours, and Nicole and the girls were asleep in the back.

"Victoria, what happened to your cheek?" Natasha asked.

"He was going to hit the girls and I stepped in between him and them. I told him it was my fault not theirs, so strike me not them, so he did, but he hit them too, and I couldn't stop him. That's when I knew I had to get them out of there," I told her, as the tears began to burn under my eyelids.

"Oh, sweetie, I am so sorry," Natasha said as she put her hand on mine. "We are almost there, I know it's a ways away, but I wanted it to be far enough away that he couldn't find you," she said.

"Thank you so much Natasha, I don't know what I would do without you, you have always been there for me," I said to her.

"You are my family, you and the three in the back are all I have, and I will do anything to protect you," Natasha said with a smile. "I also gave us a little more time. I put sleeping pills in Dominic's bottle of scotch, so that when he has his night cap, he will be out for a good 12 hours, and that gives us time," Natasha told me. How could she always think on her toes? She was always a step or two ahead me and everyone, I thought to myself.

"Thank you," I said with a smile, still very unsure of what was going on and what I was going to do.

"Here we are" she said as we drove up to a long driveway, that looked more like a two track or deer trail than a driveway. Moments later we pulled up to this rustic looking cabin. It wasn't much, but it looked decent in size, and it was safe. I woke Nicole up and, we scooped up the girls, and went inside.

Once inside the place looked like a mansion, it was beautiful. “Ok, Nicole can you take the girls upstairs, and the first room to the left is theirs, and there is an adjoining door, and that is your room,” Natasha said. “Also there are clean clothes in there for the girls, and there are towels, and soap and stuff for you in the closet, so if you want you can have a bath,” Natasha said.

“Oh, thank you madam Natasha, you are too kind.” Nicole said sincerely.

“I will be up in a minute to help with the girls,” I said.

“That’s alright madam, I will take care of them, you just relax, and take care of your cheek.” Nicole said.

“Thank you, my dear.”

“Ok, let’s look at your cheek. I want to make sure he didn’t break a tooth or cut your gum line,” Natasha said. “Here drink some of this, it will disinfect your mouth” she said, handing me a bottle of whiskey. It burned as I took a drink. “Open up and stick out your tongue” she said as she began to look in my mouth with a little flash light. “Well I don’t see any blood, or broken teeth, you’re lucky, but that cheek bone is most likely broken,” she said. “I have stuff for the pain, but there is nothing I can do about a broken cheek bone, it’s just going to have to heal,” she said.

"Natasha how did you learn about all this stuff and how are you so prepared, you have always been the carefree, wild one, and now you are the one taking care of everything?" I asked in shock.

"Well, honey, no one expects me to be prepared or responsible so no one will think anything was planned," she said. "I want you to stay here, and get some sleep. I am going to drive back, and in the morning I will go to Dominic's to see you, and then I can throw a fit, and accuse him of hurting you and the girls. Hopefully he won't suspect me of knowing anything, and I will bring some stuff back with me in the evening," Natasha said.

"Ok, but please be careful, He is dangerous, who knows what he will do," I warned.

"Dominic is no match for me," Natasha said with a laugh. Now go on up to bed, and tomorrow is a new day, a new start, she said.

"Ok, I will" I said, and hugged her good bye.

I got up and went about the house and made sure every door, window and anything else that looked like a way in, was locked or bolted shut. I really didn't want anything else to happen tonight. As I walked up the stairs, I poked my head in on the girls and Nicole. I wondered how they must be feeling right now, scared, confused, unsure of what's to come. Stephanie and Sarah were cuddled up together in one bed, and it really was a picture perfect moment. Nicole had her hand laid across Stephanie's back and her head laid down on the bed. How she loved those girls, and they loved her. I thought about waking her up, but I decided not to, she was right where she wanted to be. I looked over to the bed on the side and I decided that would be a perfect place to lie down and wait out the night, I would be close to all three of them, and they would be happy waking up and seeing me.

As I lay there in bed, I started to think about Violet, how disappointed in me she must be. I have been raising her children in a home where they can't be kids, and they go to bed fearing the man they knew as a father figure. But the girls are happy, and they know I love them, don't they? I asked myself. Well I am going to make sure they do, and they never have to be scared again, I said to myself as a promise to me and their mother. I must have laid awake for most of the night, because before I knew it, I heard Nicole begin to get restless, and it was morning and the girls were waking as well.

I nearly jumped five feet in the air, when I heard the door slam shut, I grabbed the girls and Nicole, and told them to be quiet and hide. "I am going to see who is here."

I grabbed the lamp off the dresser and began to walk quietly to the stairway, and peak down to see who it was, but I couldn't see anything. I took each step very cautiously in hopes that whoever it was wouldn't hear me. I reached the bottom of the stairs, and looked down the hallway to the kitchen, but still couldn't see anyone. I crept closer, my heart was pounding so hard, I thought whoever it was would surely hear it. I heard someone in the kitchen, so I took a deep breath and whipped open the door, and swung the lamp in hopes it would scare whoever was there, but much to my surprise it was Lord Stephan.

"Easy now Victoria, you could take someone's head off with that lamp." The sight of him there was shocking.

"How did you get in here, and how did you know I was here," I demanded to know, but I was kind of happy to see him.

"Please Victoria put the lamp down, and sit, and have some coffee," he said. I did so, and so did he.

"Now tell me why you are here," I asked.

"Natasha came to me very early this morning, earlier than the rooster crows, she told me about what happened, and asked me to come up here. She did not want you to wake up alone, and not sure of anything," he said.

"Prove it," I demanded. He held out a key, and a letter. I know her hand writing, I said, as I took the letter. I began to read it.

Victoria, I know you must be scared and worried, but I asked Stephan to come up here this morning, and bring you coffee, and make sure you were ok. I know, I swore I wouldn't tell anyone, but he has loved you since the day he met you, and he will do you or the girls no wrong. It works out good this way, because he is going on a business trip that everyone in town was aware of, including Dominic, so he won't think you ran off with him or me. So please drink your coffee, and let him drive you and the girls to your new house, it is about half a day drive. I won't get there until very early morning, or later, but I want you safe, and far away from Dominic. If you are wondering, did I really write this letter or is this a trap, well guess what? I did, so just do it, and there is a surprise under your bed that only I know about, so there is your proof.

Love you,

Natasha.

"Ok, I believe you. I am sorry I was so skeptical but I am a little on edge at the moment," I said.

"It's alright my dear," he said as he reached his hand out to move my hair off my cheek, but I jumped back. "Victoria, I would never hurt you, and you are one of my dearest friends, so please let me help." I think I jumped back more out of embarrassment of my face than anything, for I didn't want him to see what Dominic had done. "Oh my lord," he burst out as he caught a glimpse of my cheek, "what happened, Victoria, did he do that? Oh I am going to kill him, no man has the right to lay a hand on a woman, and especially leave a trail like that," he said furiously.

"Stephan please, it's not that bad, and I did it to myself," I cried.

"What do you mean not that bad, you did it to yourself," he demanded. The tears began to stream down my face as I told him what happened last night, and how I couldn't protect the girls from him, and it was my punishment for letting him strike Violets babies.

He rushed to hug me, "Victoria it is not your fault you tried to protect them, and you are protecting them by leaving. Violet would never blame you, she knows and is watching, and she is very proud of you," he said. Still holding me in his arms, I sobbed but I did feel somewhat better after what he said.

The door burst open and another lamp was being swung. It was Nicole and she had a very mean look in her eyes. Stephan, let go of me, and began to explain all over again. "Ok," she said with a smile, and said "I am going to go get the girls dressed, and bring them down for breakfast."

"Ok, Nicole" I said as I thanked her for trying to protect me.

"Madam, are you sure you are alright?" Nicole asked before she left to get the girls.

"Yes, Nicole I am alright, it has just been somewhat of an exciting morning, and I am a bit on the jumpy side." She smiled and nodded, and left to get the girls.

Moments later my phone began to ring, my heart started pounding. What if it's Dominic, what if it's Natasha and Dominic has her, panic set in, as I reached for my phone. It was indeed Dominic, my hands were trembling as I set the phone down, I couldn't answer it, I couldn't give him a chance to find us. "Relax, Victoria he doesn't know where you are, he is just calling, now calm yourself, drink some coffee, and let's get the girls fed and ready to go, we have a long drive a head of us today. Natasha will be meeting us there," Stephan said in a calming voice, that actually seemed to help.

"You're right," I said as I began to gather stuff in the kitchen for the girls.

"Lady Victoria, the girls are ready, and I hope you don't mind, I packed your things up for you," Nicole said as she and the girls entered the kitchen. To my surprise the girls were happy to see Stephan there, and especially happy to see the pastries and juice he had brought with him.

I sat there drinking my coffee, watching how the girls seemed to be relaxed and happy this morning. Maybe I am doing the right thing, I wondered, and hoped. They ate their breakfast, and were very excited about the next part of their adventure. Although Sarah was smaller than Stephanie, she was still very mature for her age, and did her role as the big sister very well. "Now Stephanie, be sure to use the potty before we leave," Sarah advised her little sister, "we have a long drive, and are only going to stop once or twice," she said.

As we started to drive, I wondered what Natasha had planned for us, was this our life now, running and hiding? I must have gotten lost in my own thoughts, because I never heard the phone ringing. "Victoria, Victoria, are you going to see who is calling?" I heard Stephan ask.

"Oh yeah, sorry I was thinking, and must have gotten lost in my own thoughts," I said with a smile. Panic seized me as I picked up the phone to see who was calling, it was Dominic again. I dropped the phone as I read the screen.

"Victoria relax, he is only calling, like I said earlier he doesn't know where you are, that's why he is calling," Stephan told me.

"Ok I know, I am just a little worried is all," I said with a smile.

"Aunt Victoria, where are we going?" Sarah asked.

"Well honey, we are going on a permanent vacation," I said.

"You know Victoria you might want to have the girls start calling you mom, because people may wonder why a woman of your class is traveling with two children who aren't hers," Stephan advised me.

"You are right about that, besides Dominic will say I am with my two nieces," I replied. "Hey girls."

"Yes Aunt Victoria," they replied.

"I have an idea, let's play a game, would you like that?" I asked.

"Yes, Yes" they cried with excitement.

"From now on let's pretend I am your mother, Stephan is your uncle, on your father's side, does that sound like fun, girls?"

"Yes, but if you are going to be our mother, who is our father?" Stephanie asked.

"Well baby, we simply tell the truth on that part. That your father, whom was my husband died in a terrible car accident, and that is why my face is the way it is," I replied. "Does that sound alright, girls?" I asked.

"Yeah, I guess, but I am confused, why are we coming up with a lie to tell people?" Stephanie asked, sounding confused..

"Well sweetie, people are going to ask questions, and depending on what Dominic thinks has happened, he may send people to find us. I don't want to go back there. He wasn't very nice to me or you guys and I promised your mother that I would always protect and take care of you girls. So that is why we need to tell a lie, if people ask" I told her, hoping she would understand, and stop asking questions.

"Ok, mom," she said with a giggle. We all laughed.

I heard a very strange ring tone, that wasn't my phone, where was it coming from? I was more curious than anything, "I think it is coming from the glove box," Stephan said. I opened the glove box and there was a phone and it was still ringing. I grabbed it, and it was Natasha.

"Hello," I answered kind of cautiously.

"Hey how are you? It's me, Natasha."

"Oh, hey we are good, thank you so much for everything," I said with a sigh of relief.

"Ok, enough chit chat, where about are you right now?" she asked, with a demanding tone.

"I believe we are coming up to I-16 in about 1 mile," I said.

"Good you are right on schedule. Ok, get on I-16 and inside the glove box is a map. Read and memorize it, that will lead you to the house, and let Stephan hang on to it. Also there is another map in there, I want you to stop and ask for directions, at the second gas station you come to, and use the second map when you talk to the cashier. And this part is critical, there is a rest stop right before you get on the interstate, stop there and there is a different vehicle parked in the back. It has a full tank of gas, food, and clothes and everything you will need, including another map for you and Stephan. But please, once you reach the other car have Stephan take it and you continue in the same car. He can't stop at the gas station with you, he will be waiting at the 3rd exit after the gas station, remember the 3rd exit after the gas station," she said in more of a panicky tone than I have ever heard her use.

"Ok, but what is going on? You sound terrified," I said.

"I will explain when I get there, at the 3rd exit after the gas station. Leave the car there, be sure to leave a few minor items in it, so Dominic knows you were in it. But take the map that I asked you to use at the gas station, leave the map slightly tucked under the tire, or shut in the door. Be sure it looks like you accidently left it in there," she said.

"Ok, I will do it, and I promise, but please promise me you will be ok," I begged her.

"I will, I promise, just please hurry and get to the destination," she said.

"Ok, I will."

"There's the rest stop, ok now, what are we suppose to do Victoria?" Stephan asked.

"Ok, there is a car parked in back, you take that car and I will take this one, I need to stop at the second gas station, and I will meet you at the 3rd exit after the gas station. We will join you in that car, we need to leave a few minor items in the car, and leave the second map but make it look like it was accidently left," I told Stephan.

"Ok, let's get to it," he said.

"Victoria, madam what is happening now?" Nicole asked with a worried tone of voice.

"It's ok honey, everything is going to be fine," I said in a calm somewhat soothing voice, hoping to ease her mind. The poor girl has been through so much.

"Ok, madam," she replied, more calm now.

I saw the gas station, and I began to pull in, and watched through the rear view mirror to see if Stephan went on by. He did, relief set in for a moment. I grabbed the map, and went inside and I asked the cashier if she could help me. She did, but she was kind of suspicious acting, and kept looking outside. After she gave me directions, I thanked her and left, and made sure I pulled out as Natasha said. I met Stephan at the 3rd exit and placed the map in an accidental place.

We were back on the road, and we followed the map just as she advised. The girls fell asleep in the back seat, but they really seemed to enjoy most of ride. It took a few hours but we got there. It was a little town, but it was cozy. "I wonder where we are at, I have never been here before," I thought out loud.

"There it is, Victoria" Stephan said. It was a very cute house, it looked just like every house in town, and it was at the end of the road, so it was private, but very close to everything.

"Girls, wake up we are here," I said with a sigh of relief.

"Victoria, why don't you gather the girls up and I will unlock the door, and just make a quick check to be sure everything is ok, and there are no surprises inside," Stephan said.

"Ok, thank you," I said.

A few moments later Stephan came out and we gathered our belongings and went inside. The house was perfect for what we needed, 3 bedrooms, and a master bedroom, with a master bathroom. There was a very large kitchen, with a huge deck through the sliding window. For the first time in a very long time, I felt safe, but how long would it last?

"Victoria? It's Natasha, she's on the phone," Stephan said.

"Ok, hey how are you, are you ok?" I asked, in hopes she would say she was almost here.

"I'm fine, I just wanted to make sure you and the girls were alright," she said.

"Yes, we are all ok, why did you sound so worried, and scared earlier?" I asked.

"I will tell you when I get there, but please do me a favor. Put the car in the garage, and lock every door, window, anything that could possibly let someone in the house, and garage," she asked.

"Yes I will, when are you going to be here?" I asked.

"I will be there in a few hours, there is food in the cupboards so you can make the girls and yourself something to eat," she said.

"Ok, please be careful," I said.

"I will," she said.

"Hey, girls what would you like for dinner?" I yelled up to them from the bottom of the stairs. All three of them came running down. They all seemed very happy, even Nicole, whom I had never seen smile as much as she was today.

"Can we have hotdogs?" Stephanie asked.

"Yeah I think hotdogs would be good tonight, how does that sound Sarah, Nicole?"

"That's fine with us," they replied. "Can we have mac and cheese with it too, please?" they begged as they stuck their lips out all pouty like.

"Yes, I love mac and cheese," I said, "why don't you girls go up and get changed, and I will start dinner.

"Ok, we will," they yelled, as they ran up the stairs.

"Victoria, are you alright?" Stephan asked as he put his hand on the small of my back.

"Yes, I am, I am very alright at the moment, all the girls are happy, even Nicole. She has always seemed so distant, and shy before, but today I saw a difference in her, and I am happy. I feel like she too is my daughter and I will treat her just as that," I said with a smile. "So, Sir Stephan how do you like your hotdog?" I asked with a giggle.

"I wondered what made the girls want a hotdog for dinner, but it did sound good. I hadn't had a hotdog since I was a child. I think I would like my hotdog with ketchup, mustard, and pickles," he replied with a giggle. "You, know Victoria, I haven't had a hotdog since I was a little boy, and for some reason it sounds wonderful tonight," he said with a laugh. I looked through the cupboards, and found the mac and cheese, and there were hotdogs in the fridge.

While making dinner I wondered if this was the end of all the pain and sorrow in the girls and my life, would we be happy? Would Dominic not look for us? I hoped all would be good. Stephan began setting the table, and looking for condiments for our hotdogs. "Girls, I called up the stairs, dinner is done, so please come down here."

Moments later they came down the stairs, and sat down at the table. I put the dinner on the table and Stephan and I sat down too.

"Dinner is very good, Mom" Sarah said. It sounded so weird to be called mom, but I knew it would be the only way to hopefully pull our story off.

After dinner I cleared the table and dishes, I couldn't believe how late it was. I decided it was time to put the girls to bed, so I went upstairs and both girls were sound asleep. Nicole was sitting in the rocking chair asleep herself. As I went to tuck Stephanie in she opened her eyes, and gave me hug, and said thank you for everything, I almost started to cry. How happy it made me feel that she was happy, I had hoped this wouldn't scare them. I began to tuck in Sarah and she too opened her eyes, and told me good night and she loved me.

As I went to wake Nicole to tell her she could go to bed, she nearly hit me as she swung her arms when I touched her shoulder, "easy sweetie it's me Victoria, the girls are asleep, why don't you go to bed yourself? I will be in here with them for awhile, and this is home now. We are safe, so you can relax," I said to her in hopes she would relax, and be a kid herself.

"Ok, Madam, I will, but if you need me I will just be in the next room," she said.

"Ok darling, but please get some rest."

"I will thank you," she said as she went to her room.

I heard the door open, and before I knew I was running down the stairs with a lamp in my hand, ready to swing it on whoever was coming through the door, but as I reached the door, it was Natasha. I dropped the lamp and ran to her, "are you ok?" I asked as I wrapped my arms around her to hug her.

"Yes, I am good, are you and the girls ok?" she asked.

"Yes we are, they are sound asleep, and happy," I said as tears began to run down my cheeks.

"Hey why are you crying?" Natasha asked.

"Because I was so worried about you," I replied stilling crying. "So, why did you sound so frantic earlier on the phone? And please don't tell me you were just worried." I said as more of a demand than a question.

"Ok, but it's not facts, it's what I heard, so it may not be true," she said.

"Ok. I understand that," I replied.

"I was told that Dominic's stepmother mysteriously died, a few months after his father died of a heart attack, leaving her all of his assets, including all the money," she said.

"Did they say how she died?" I asked.

"Yes, apparently she fell down the stairs, and was in a coma, but the last one to see her at the house was Dominic. He was also the last one to see her alive at the hospital," she said.

"Was there an investigation, or anything?" I asked with fear dripping in my voice.

"Yes, there was, but it got dropped shortly after. There was a large donation to the sheriff's department, and all the evidence they had, miraculously disappeared," she said.

"What? It all disappeared? Was there anything leading them to Dominic?" I asked.

"Yes, she had skin under her fingernails, and the DNA matched Dominic's, but no one knows if that is true or not. After I heard that I knew you were in more danger than we thought," she said.

"OK, I understand that but, what was with the gas station thing?" I asked.

"Well, I was at my house, getting ready for the meeting I had, and Dominic showed up with six other guys, three of which were in uniform. They started asking me questions, and I overheard Dominic on the phone with someone, telling them the make, model, and license plate number of the vehicle. I knew then that he had people looking, so that's when I came up with a plan to give them something to follow, and I arranged for someone to find the car, and lead Dominic on a wild goose chase." As she was telling me this, panic came over me.

"What am I going to do if he finds me?" I asked her.

"Relax, he isn't going to find you, have faith," she said.

"Ok, ladies, I'm sorry to interrupt your moment of terror, and panic, but if you hadn't noticed it's really late. Sarah, Stephanie, and Nicole are asleep and happy for the first time in a long time, so can we please relax, and not fret tonight? We can stress in the morning, but tonight Victoria needs some rest, and probably some ice or whiskey for that cheek of hers" Stephan said.

"Ok, Stephan, but there is something else I need to tell her, and this can't wait," Natasha said to him.

"Ok, well Natasha tell her, if it's something that important than you need to tell her now," he said. I heard fear in his voice, and that wasn't a tone I was used to hearing out of him.

"Ok, Victoria I heard Dominic talking to a bank about a safe deposit box, and there is a letter from someone to you in that box. He told the man to burn the letter, everything would be lost if you found that letter." When she said that, I remembered him talking about a safe deposit box before.

"Did he happen to mention where the bank was?" I asked in hopes she would know.

"Yes, and I went to that bank and I received your letter," she said.

"What? How did you get it? What did you do?" I asked.

"Well I reminded the bank that I had more money, and assets in their bank than any other person there. And if he didn't do what I needed I would take everything out of there, and make sure everyone else did as well. As I figured he gave up the box."

"OK, so where is the letter?" I asked.

"Right here, but Victoria please be cautious, I have no clue what that letter is about, and if it's from Dominic god only knows what he is going to do when he realizes it's gone," she said with worry dripping off every word.

I began to open the letter, curious yet very scared of what I might find. As I took the letter out I looked up at

Natasha and Stephan, how lucky I was to have them in my life, and here for me when I needed them.

Dear Victoria,

You have no clue who I am, and I am sorry I was never there for you, but I always knew how you were doing. I wrote the orphanage every other week to see how you and your sister were. I know you and Violet were very close, and I know you have her two beautiful little girls, Sarah and Stephanie. That was a wonderful thing you did for your sister. If you are reading this letter now, then I have passed away, and I have left you and your sister my entire estate. Since Violet has passed away, you will receive her part of my estate, since you have her children and will be caring for them. I know you married a very wealthy man, Dominic Huntsmen, but you need to know he is a very evil man, and if he ever gets a hold of this letter, there is a chance your life could be in danger, and the girls as well. I wrote your half sister a letter as well, but in her letter she has no clue she has two sisters, and she knows she received a ton of money when I passed, but there is that much plus more left to you. I hope you don't hate me for never being around but when I heard my daughter was with child, I snapped and yelled at her and kicked her out. She left, but never returned, and then I got sick, and realized I had no one, I tried to call her. And that's when I found out she had died, and I thought my life was over when I heard that. I decided I would find you and your sister, but when I did I realized I was too far gone to care for you, so I left you in the orphanage but I kept in contact until I died. All you need to do is call your half sister to find out the name of the bank where your inheritance is, but remember she doesn't know she has a sister. However, the bank does, and they will take care of everything, so please call this number and reach your half sister, I hope by the time you get this letter it's not too late, here's the number 569-2202. One more thing, a day never went by that I didn't love you, or regret my getting mad at your mother, but we are in heaven together now, and we have mended fences. I love you, and live your life like there is no tomorrow.

All my love, Your Grandfather, Joseph Strong

"Oh my goodness, Natasha I have another sister, and a ton of money. This letter is from my grandfather."

"What? that's wonderful honey," she said as she hugged me. I have another sister too, there is a number to call her, what should I do? I asked.

"Call her," they both said with anticipation.

"Ok, I will. Stephan can I use your phone?" I asked.

"Of course," he said as he handed it to me.

My hands were trembling as I began to dial the number, “oh it’s ringing”, I gasped.

“Oh just a second” Natasha said, “my phone is ringing, I hope It’s not Dominic.”

I said. “Hello?” someone answered, “um hi, my name is Victoria,” I said, but it was silent. “Hello,” I repeated.

“Victoria?” Natasha said as she was giving me a strange look.

“What is it, Natasha? I asked.

“You called me,” she said as we both hung up the phone, in confusion.

“What? I called you?” I said. “What does that mean?” I asked her.

“I’m not sure,” she replied. We were both silent for a few moments.

“Natasha? What was your grandfather’s name?” Stephan asked.

“Oh, um it was Joseph Strong,” she said.

“Are you sure Natasha?” I asked with anticipation.

“Yes, I’m positive,” she said.

“That is who this letter is from,” I said. We all were in shock. All this time Natasha and I had been sisters and very wealthy and never knew it. I handed Natasha the letter, so she could read it.

"This calls for a celebration" Stephan declared as he grabbed a bottle of wine and three glasses. I still couldn't believe this, but what did he mean when he said my life would be in danger if Dominic knew about this letter? I thought.

"Ok, let's not get too ahead of ourselves," I said. "We still have Dominic to worry about," I reminded them.

"Victoria, tomorrow we will drive to the bank, and show them this letter, and go from there," Natasha said. She was always so level headed, and always had a plan.

"Ok, you're right," I said as I took a glass from Stephan, and we all toasted to new beginnings. We sipped our wine, all of us were still in shock it seemed, but it was good. "I am going to go to bed, but I am going to stay in the girl's room," I said.

"Ok, good night Victoria, please get some sleep" Stephan said. Natasha stood up and hugged me, how nice it was that she was my sister, we have always been more like sisters, but to be actually sisters was something out of this world, I thought.

The next morning came too fast. I woke up to Sarah and Stephanie jumping on the bed, yelling good morning

Mom. I wondered if they had always thought of me as mom, but were too afraid to say it. I got up and put on some clothes. I helped the girls get dressed, and I gave Nicole one of the outfits I had packed so she had a new outfit for today. "Miss Victoria you didn't need to do that," she said as she hugged me.

"I know dear, but you always help me and you always have," I said. "Ok girls, I am going to go down and make breakfast, so why don't you guys make your beds and brush your teeth, while I do that," I said.

"Ok, we will."

Downstairs, Stephan and Natasha were already up, and had coffee poured. "Thank you guys, I was just coming to do that," I said.

"Ok, here is the plan," Natasha declared as she told us about the bank, and where to go.

"Wow, Natasha did you sleep at all last night, or were you up planning everything?" I asked with a giggle.

"Well you know, I have never been a good sleeper," she replied with a giggle.

"Girls? Breakfast," I called to them, and they immediately came down the stairs and began to eat their breakfast. "Girls, we have a long day planned, so if you would like you can stay here with Nicole or you can all come with us," I said.

"We want to stay with Nicole" they chanted. Nicole even seemed happy about that idea.

"Ok, well Natasha, and I need to go to the bank," I said, "and you better listen to Nicole, she's in charge," I said sternly.

"Ok, we will, we promise," they said.

"Victoria, can I talk to you in private for a moment?" Stephan asked.

"Of course, Stephan," I said. We went upstairs, so we could talk. Once upstairs, he looked very puzzled, and confused.

"Victoria, if you don't mind I would like to stick around for a while, to help make sure you are all ok. I know you don't need it, but I care deeply about you, and the girls, and hell even Natasha. I have no reason to go home, if you're not there," he said.

"Oh, Stephan, of course you can. I would really like that, but I want you to know, I can only be friends with you. I am still married, and there is too much happening. I need to focus on the girls, and keeping Dominic from us," I said. The thought of hurting Stephan made me sick to my stomach, but I couldn't tell him how I really felt, for if

Dominic found us together he would kill him, just to make me suffer.

"I know Victoria, you have always been a good friend and that's the reason, I am here," he said.

"Ok, thank you, Stephan you are the best," I said as I hugged him, and turned to go back to the girls and Natasha.

"Stephan, are you coming?" I asked.

"Yes, I will be right there," he said. If she only knew I have loved her since the day I met her, if she only knew I could keep her safe, and I would never hurt her, Stephan said to himself.

"Ok, Victoria, are you ready to go?" Natasha asked with anticipation for today.

"Yes," I said.

"Ok, let's do this," Natasha said with a nervous giggle. As we walked outside I noticed more of the area, it looked really familiar, but we drove for so long yesterday, and we took roads I have never been on before.

"Natasha, what town are we in? it looks familiar," I asked.

"Oh, we are in a small town about an hour or so from home," she replied.

"Really, why did it take so long to get here?" I asked confused.

"Well, I knew Dominic would send people to follow us, so I wanted to get him as far away as possible and sneak you back closer. So when I need to return home for something, I can, and my bank is here, well our bank is here," she said.

"That reminds me, Natasha, should we consider getting a different bank so Dominic can't trace it?" I asked.

"Yes, we will, but first let's figure out the situation at hand, your money and estate," she said with a smile so sweet, hoping it would relax me. It did kind of, with her at my side I know everything will be ok; she gives me strength to do what I need to.

Natasha was right; the bank was right in town, it was right next to a bakery, and a little boutique.

"Ok, Victoria, when we go inside, we will ask to speak to the manager and tell him it is a very sensitive matter, and we are trusting him to be discreet. Once we are in his office, we will tell him our grandfather's name, and present him the letter. Since he knows me, it should go smoothly, but we need to be prepared for him to ask about Dominic. We will tell him that Dominic is a very powerful man, and dangerous for that matter. If he doesn't comply with our wishes we will make sure Dominic knows who gave us the letter, from Dominic's safe deposit box, and that should scare the crap out of the banker," she said.

"Ok, Natasha let's do this, and hurry home to the girls," I said.

"They will be fine, Victoria, now focus, we need to be sure this goes right and in our favor, we can't risk Dominic finding out you have the letter," she demanded.

"I know, I know, I'm sorry, I'm just worried is all," I said trying to pull myself together.

We walked up to the entrance, and Natasha opened the door, gesturing me to enter first. I walked through, and she walked in and took the lead towards the customer service desk. There was a little old lady sitting in her chair. She had almost pure gray hair, and a face as round as an apple, with small round glasses sitting on her nose. "How may I help you today?" she asked with a very sweet smile.

"Hello, we would like to speak to the manager or someone in charge. It is very urgent and a very sensitive matter, if you don't mind," Natasha said to the woman.

"Ok, I will get the manager for you, please have a seat," she said as she pointed to the chairs in the lobby area.

"Thank you ma'am," Natasha said, as we turned to have a seat. Moments later a fairly tall man, who looked to be in his early to mid fifties, appeared.

"Oh, well good morning Ms. Natasha, how are you today? What can I do for you?" he said.

"Hello, Mr. Wellington, this is my friend Victoria; remember we spoke yesterday about a letter, in Mr. Huntsmen's safe deposit box?" Natasha said with a very stern, commanding look on her face.

"Oh yes, please ladies if you could just follow me, we can discuss this in my office," he said with a look, that almost looked frightened by Natasha's words.

Once we entered his office, Mr. Wellington's demeanor changed, he seemed less professional, and almost scared. "Mr. Wellington are you alright? you seem very worried," I asked.

"Yes, I'm sorry, but Natasha here, knows how much trouble I am in if Dominic finds out you have that letter, it is very possible he could kill me," he said.

"Well, maybe he doesn't have to know. You see I have the letter with me, and once we do our business, I can simply give you a copy of the letter, and put it back in the original envelope. That way when Dominic wants to know you can prove to him you have it still," I said with a shocking level of confidence, that I surprised even myself.

"You know, Victoria, that is a great idea, don't you think, Mr. Wellington?" Natasha asked.

"Yes, I do think that is a great idea," he said with relief.

"Ok, can we please get to the point of our meeting? It seems I have an inheritance of money, and an estate I would like to claim," I said with very sternly. "I don't mean to be, rude or unpleasant, but I am in a hurry. Dominic is looking for me, and if he finds me or my girls, we are dead. And if he knows about this letter, than he is already planning my funeral, so if you don't mind, let's get the paperwork started, and let me get out of here, please," I demanded.

"Yes, ma'am I'm sorry, may I see the letter please? just for identification purposes, to verify you are who you say you are," Mr. Wellington said.

"Please, Mr. Wellington, you know damn well who she is, so get the paperwork, and give her, the correct information, or we will call Dominic right now, and tell him how you deceived him," Natasha ordered.

"Ok, Victoria here is a copy of the account number, and an address for the estate. Here is a sealed letter, from your grandfather, that I assure you no one knows about," he said.

"Ok, where do I sign," I asked.

"Actually, you don't need to sign, I believe your Grandfather set it up that way so there wouldn't be a paper trail," he said.

"I hate to bother you, with my own problems, but there is still the matter of the letter, and your husband Victoria," he said cautiously.

"Yes, where is the copier? and I will make a copy for you," I asked.

"Right this way," he said as he led the way.

"Here is your copy, and if there is a problem of Dominic finding out that we are here, I will be sure to inform him, where I got the letter, and how we set it up so you wouldn't get caught Mr. Wellington," I said with a sharpness in my tone.

As we got into the car I opened the letter, and all it was, was an address and a key. "Natasha what do I do with this?"

"Well, let's go get the girls and go find out," Natasha said.

"Ok, let's do it, but what if it's a trap, what if Dominic set it up so he could trick us into thinking we were safe, and then he sneaks in and hurts the girls, me or even you?" I asked fear dripping off every word.

"Victoria, look at the hand writing, and then look at the hand writing of your letter, if they match then relax, do they match Dominic's?" Natasha asked.

"No, they don't," I said with a little more relief.

"Ok then, now can we focus on what to do next?" Natasha asked.

"Yes, I am sorry, I shouldn't have panicked."

As we pulled down the road, I noticed a strange car sitting in the driveway. "Whose car is that in the driveway?" I yelled, panic had seized me completely. My heart began to race, and all I could think of was Dominic sitting inside holding my babies, with Stephan laid out on the floor in his own blood, and poor Nicole, beaten within inches of her life. "Oh my goodness, Natasha what are we going to do? What if it's Dominic?" I cried.

"Victoria, relax I don't think it is Dominic, but to be safe, I have a plan," she said calmly. "Open the glove box," she ordered. "There is a colt 45 in there, but be careful it's loaded. Now I am going to park up the road just past the house, and I am going to sneak in through the kitchen and you are going to go in through the front, like nothing is going on. Now give me the gun, I don't want you rushing in the front door, waving a gun around," she said more as an order than a statement.

"Now remember, be calm when you open the door, but be prepared," Natasha advised.

"Ok, I can do it," I said, just breathe just breathe, I repeated to myself as I grabbed the handle of the door, and turned it to open, and hope I am wrong.

"Victoria, how are you?" a man asked me.

"Who are you, and how the hell did you get in this house, why are you here, who sent you?" I demanded, I could feel the fire building inside me.

"Get away from her you son of"

"Well hello to you to, my dear," the man said as Natasha held the gun up to him, forcing him to turn around.

"Luke, how are you?" Natasha said as she set the gun down, and wrapped her arms around him, and kissed him on the lips.

"Hey, Natasha who is this man, and why the hell is he here?" I demanded.

"Oh, I'm sorry, Victoria this is my friend Luke, I called him yesterday and told him what was going on, I guess I forgot to tell you that I have been seeing someone," she said.

"Natasha can I see you in the kitchen please?" I asked.

"What are you thinking, telling someone where we are?" I asked. "How well do you know this man, can we trust him?" I asked.

"Ok, Victoria I understand you are upset, but please trust me, I haven't know him that long, but we have been seeing each other for a few months now," she said. "Victoria relax, I haven't told him everything, I only told him, you ran away from Dominic because he is a very evil man, and you are scared for the life of you and the girls. He understood, but that is all I told him, and I won't tell him anything else, I promise," she said.

"Ok, I'm sorry I panicked, but there has been so much that has happened I am just jumpy," I said.

"Ok, now can we please go back to the living room, and be polite to our guest, and maybe you could possibly get to know him? for me please?" she asked in a very sincere voice.

"Ok, let's go," I said as I turned to go back to the living room.

"Luke is it?" I asked as I held out my hand to properly introduce myself to him.

"Yes, its Luke" he said, accepting my hand.

"Please forgive my rudeness, I am a little stressed and overwhelmed today, and I hope you accept my invitation to dinner tonight, and my sincerest apology," I said.

"Thank you ma'am, I would be honored to have dinner tonight, but I apologize I can't stay late, I must be getting back tonight, I have a very important business deal in the morning that I need to prep for," he said.

"What kind of business do you do?" I asked, more out of an interrogation than interest.

"Actually, I am a lawyer, and tomorrow I am meeting with a very important client, so I must prepare, and get my portfolio in order," he said.

"How long have you been practicing law?" I asked?

"Oh, I think it has been about five years. It was always my father's dream for me. Mine was to be an artist, but I decided to go forth with law, once father got ill, and passed away," he said.

"Oh, I'm sorry, I didn't mean to pry, or bring up sad memories," I said.

"No, it's ok, I have made peace with it," he said.

"Well, Victoria what do you have planned for dinner?" Stephan asked. I think it was more to change the subject so I would stop interrogating Luke.

"I was thinking chicken, how does that sound?" I replied?

"That sounds wonderful," they all said.

"Victoria, why don't I help you in the kitchen with dinner and give these two some privacy?" Stephan said.

"That is a wonderful idea Stephan," I said as we got up and went to start dinner. "Stephan, I don't like this, I don't like Luke, he's hiding something, and I'm not sure what, but I don't trust him," I began ranting.

"Easy Victoria you are just stressed and you are scared, but that doesn't mean he is a bad guy," he said.

"Ok, I'm sorry, I will relax, but I still think he is suspicious," I declared.

"Victoria, why do you think Dominic is behind this?" he asked.

"It's his voice, it sounds very familiar," I replied.

"Ok, but have you ever seen that man before? he asked.

"No, but…"

"No, Victoria, no buts, you don't know him, and if you truly care for Natasha you will keep your opinion to yourself, and wait until you have proof, before you accuse," he said in a very stern voice.

"Ok, I will, but if I am right he will regret the day he ever met Dominic," I said in a voice that startled even me.

"Hey, why don't you go get the girls ready for dinner and I will finish up in here?" he said.

"Ok, thank you." I was truly lucky to have him in my life, I thought as I went upstairs to get the children ready.

When I got upstairs to see my girls, to my surprise they were playing candy land with Nicole. They looked like normal little girls being good, and playing. "So who's winning?" I asked as I entered the room.

"It's a pretty close game so far," Sarah said,

"but I think Stephanie might actually win," Nicole declared.

"Well girls, is there any way you guys can finish this game after dinner, because dinner will be done shortly, and I would like you to get ready?" I asked.

"Ok, we will. No cheating Sarah," Stephanie said.

"I won't," she spat.

"Ok, girls no fighting, let's get cleaned up now please."

"Ok, I will make sure they are down in a few minutes," Nicole said.

"Thank you, Nicole, but sweetie do you know, you are not a baby sitter or maid here, you are like my daughter, just as Sarah, and Stephanie. So please don't think you have to take care of them nonstop, believe me I appreciate the help, but I don't expect it," I said.

"Thank you, Victoria, and I think of you more of a mom than a boss, I always have, you have always kept me safe from Dominic, and now it's my turn to help you," she said and hugged me. I felt the tears burning behind my eyelids, but I held them back, I know if she sees me cry she will do the same.

"Sorry to interrupt, but dinner is done," I went to the living room and told Natasha and Luke.

"Ok, Victoria we will be in, in just a second," Natasha said with a giggle. I had never seen Natasha act like a google eyed school girl before, and I wasn't sure I liked seeing it at this moment.

As I stepped into the kitchen I overheard, Luke say something, about where we're headed tomorrow, but Natasha didn't tell him, she said we were staying there near her bank, and somewhat close to our town. I was happy with her response to him, I couldn't help but being cautious right now, and until I was certain Luke wasn't working for

Dominic, I wasn't going to take any chances with him, and hopefully Natasha understands that.

"Oh, wow Victoria this chicken is wonderful, I would've never guessed you were such an amazing cook," Luke said.

"Why is that Luke? Why would you assume I couldn't cook?" I asked, maybe a little too sharply?

"Oh, I meant no disrespect, it is just, Natasha has told me about the wonderful meals, your former cook has prepared. So I assumed you have always had a wonderful chef, and never been made to cook," he said.

"I didn't mean to snap at you Luke, I was just shocked by your statement. I was curious as to what made you think that, but thank you very much for the compliments on dinner," I said, hoping to end this discussion. I did not want to upset Natasha, she has always been there for me, and I knew it was important to her, for me to be supportive.

"Well, I hate to eat and run, but it is getting late, and I must get started home, but again thank you for having me this evening, and thank you for a wonderful dinner Victoria," Luke said.

"Here I will walk you out, Luke," Natasha said as they got up to leave. I couldn't help but notice how Luke avoided eye contact with me, it was almost like he didn't want me to know something, or see something.

I couldn't help but try to listen to them, and I must have made it obvious, because Stephan told me to stop, and relax. "I am sorry, would anyone like more chicken?" I asked.

"No, thank you, may we be excused?" Sarah asked.

"Yes, girls, why don't you go on upstairs and get ready for bed, and then finish your game. I will be up in few to tuck you in," I said. I could hear them talking all the way up the stairs, about who was going to win the game.

"Victoria, are you ok?" Stephan asked?

"Yeah, I am I am just worried is all," I said with a sigh. I cleared the dishes, Stephan helped silently, I think he knew it was best to just let me be right now.

"Victoria, can I talk to you for a moment?" Natasha asked as she came back into the kitchen.

"Yeah, of course," I said trying to sound like everything was good.

"Thank you for trying to be nice but honey I know you are scared, and I promise you I will and would never do anything to put you or the girls in jeopardy," she said.

"I know. I am just so scared of Dominic finding us, that I kind of forgot you need certain things as well, so I am sorry and I will be more accepting to Luke if he makes you happy," I said.

"Thank you Victoria, I love you, and the girls, and I am sorry if I made you scared or worry more," she said as we hugged.

"Would anyone like a glass of Merlot this evening?" Stephan said as he carried 3 glasses of wine out.

"I think that sounds wonderful, Stephan thank you," I said. I told Stephan about the address, and key that was in the envelope we received from the bank today, and how we were planning on finding it tomorrow morning.

"Do you guys mind if I come along or do you think it would be best if I went home for the night?" Stephan asked.

"Honestly, Stephan, I would love it if you came with us, but by now Dominic is thinking you and Victoria are together. So maybe you should go home, and make up a story, about your business meeting, and the new property you bought on the other side of the state, to start a new business," Natasha said.

"That does sound like a good idea, and maybe you could swing by Dominic's so it doesn't look like you don't know Victoria has left," she said.

"Wow, Natasha you have this all figured out, don't you?" he said.

"Actually yes, my plan has changed dramatically since I found out about our grandfather, but I think it will work better now," she said with a smile.

"I am tired you guys, so I think I am going to go tuck the girls in, and then head to bed myself. I am exhausted and I think this wine is starting to hit me," I said.

"Ok, Victoria, get some sleep, if you don't mind I will come up in a few minutes to check on things before I head home," Stephan said.

"Ok, thank you. Natasha, are you going to sleep down here or are you going to go up stairs?" I asked.

"I'm not sure, I think I am going to surf the web for a few minutes, and try to find that address for tomorrow," she said.

"Ok, well good night," I said as I hugged and thanked her.

The girls were already asleep, just like last night, so I kissed them good night, and pulled up their blankets, and went to check on Nicole. "Nicole? are you sleeping, sweetie?" I asked.

"No, ma'am I was thinking I would take a bath, if you don't mind?" she asked.

"Of course my dear, you take a bath and relax, I just checked on the girls and they are asleep. I am going to bed, I just wanted to make sure you were alright," I said.

"I am good, it's nice to see the girls happy and being children for once," she said.

"I know. I love seeing those little smiles, and hearing the mischievous little giggles," I said with a giggle myself. "Well good night dear; if you need anything please let me know," I said as I hugged her good night.

As I was changing into my pajamas, I didn't hear Stephan come up the stairs, and I was startled to see him in the doorway, while I was standing there in my bra and panties. I grabbed my blanket to cover myself, as my face reddened. "I'm sorry, I wasn't trying to look, but when I saw you, you just looked so beautiful, I lost my words for a moment," he said as his face turned redder than mine. I was hoping he didn't see the scar or the bruises I tried to cover up. I have always loved him, and wanted him in intimate ways, but I knew I couldn't risk his life, just to please myself.

"It's alright, just give me a moment to dress," I said with a blushing smile that I couldn't hide. He turned and went into the hallway while I dressed.

"It's ok to come in now." I went to the door and said letting him know I was dressed.

"Victoria I hope you don't mind but I would like to stay until you fall asleep," he said more as a question than anything.

"Stephan, I would like that" I said. I hated the idea of him leaving, but I knew it was for the best. "Well you don't have to stand, you can sit," I said as I sat on the bed, hoping he would too.

"Ok," he said as he sat on the bed with me. "Victoria do you remember when we were just kids, and I used to come and see you every morning after breakfast?" he asked.

"Yes, I do. I also remember after breakfast we would run down to the river and pretend we were pirates pushing each other into the water," I said as I had to laugh. "things were always so easy as a kid with you around," I said.

"I miss those times," he said. "I also remember you were my first kiss," he said as he put his hand on my leg.

"You were mine as well, you were also the first guy I saw naked. Do you remember the first time we snuck out, and went swimming at midnight? Of course we forgot our swim suits, so we each undressed behind a tree, and went running into the water, in hopes we wouldn't see each other?" I said remembering it like it was yesterday.

"Yes, I do remember that Victoria. I also remember you screaming when you felt a snake or stick graze your leg. Well I have a confession, it wasn't a snake or a stick, it was me. Apparently you had an uncontrollable effect on me back then, that I didn't understand," he said with a blushing smile.

"I have a confession too," I said. "I knew it was you that night because when the moonlight was shining so bright on the water, I could see it," I said, turning completely red.

"Oh, so you knew that, and wanted me to think you were scared of snakes in the water," he said as he laughed.

I laughed too, "I only did that so you wouldn't get embarrassed and stop coming around," I said with a shy giggle.

I couldn't help but yawn, "why don't you lie down, and I will sit in the chair until you fall asleep?" he said.

"You don't have to sit in the chair you can lay next to me," I said as I started to lie down. As we lay there next to each other, I couldn't help but want him to stay.

"Victoria, you are doing the right thing, by running from Dominic, he is a very evil man, and you and the girls deserve to be safe," he said.

"Thank you, Stephan but I can't help being scared of what he will do. I know he is very powerful, and evil. If he finds me, he will kill me," I said, the tears starting to come down my cheeks.

"Hey, don't cry, it will be ok," he said wrapping his arms around me. "Victoria, look at me please," he said. "you are a beautiful, strong, powerful woman, and you will be ok. If he does find you, I promise you he will not hurt you again, I will see to it myself," he said as he leaned closer. I couldn't help leaning closer. There has always been this magnetic pull to him. As I leaned closer, so did he, and once our lips were touching, I felt this electric tingling sensation all over my body. "Victoria?" he said,

"Yes Stephan, I love you, I have always have. Oh Stephan," I said.

"No please don't say anything, I know we are friends and right now that's all we can be, but I wanted you to know, you are loved, and cared for," he said while holding me close.

"Thank you, Stephan." I wanted so bad to feel him closer to me, but I knew if I did, it could get him killed. We both lay there awake for a while, but I must have fallen asleep because when I woke he was gone. There was a note telling me good morning, and he would see me tonight, I had to smile when I read that.

I went down to make coffee and I saw Natasha sound asleep on the sofa. I tiptoed into the kitchen to make coffee and breakfast. I was still thinking about Stephan, and I never heard the kitchen door open, and before I knew it, I was getting thrown across the kitchen by a man in a black ski mask. I hit the fridge so hard, I felt my ribs break. I screamed hoping it would wake Natasha. I grabbed the coffee pot and threw it at him. It hit him, and I could see it pissed him off, because he grabbed me again and pushed me up against the wall. I started kicking and hitting him, hoping he would let me go. I never saw Natasha come into the kitchen, and neither did he. She hit him in the back of the head with a skillet, and he let go of me, sending me very fast and hard to the floor. He turned and pushed her, sending her backwards a few feet and ran out the door.

"Oh my goodness, Victoria you are bleeding," she said as she helped me up. I was bleeding from the side of my head near my eye.

"I think my ribs are broken," I said as I gasped for air.

“How did he get in here?” she asked.

“I don’t know” I replied still trying to catch my breath. I was lost in my thoughts and never heard the door open, I said. Panic seized me as I remember the girls were upstairs. “I must get the girls,” I yelled and went running up the stairs. Nicole was in their room, holding a baseball bat, with them behind her. She is very protective of us, I am so lucky to have her, I thought. “Are you guys ok?” I asked as I hugged them.

“Yes, we are. Are you ok ma’am?” she asked, noticing the blood and bruises, starting to appear.

“Yes, I am let’s get our things together and get out of here,” I said.

“Ok, I will get the girls,” she said.

"Ok, thank you.”

Natasha already had everything packed up of ours, and was loading the car, “wow you move fast Natasha,” I said.

“Well, we need to, if he has found us already, than he is smarter than we thought,” she said. “How are the girls?” she asked.

“They are fine. Nicole is gathering their things,” I said as I heard them coming down the stairs.

"The girls and I are ready, Victoria," Nicole said as they entered the kitchen and saw the mess.

"Nicole, it's ok, can you put the girls in the car please?" I asked.

"Yes I will," she said, looking at me for answers. I nodded to her to take them to the car, and she did so.

"Victoria, let's go," Natasha said, "grab the letters" she said as we walked out to the car.

The girls and Nicole were quiet for some time while we were driving. "Natasha did you ever figure out where that address was at?" I asked trying to break the silence.

"Actually yes, I did it's in a small town in Rhode Island," she said.

"How long will it take to get there?"

"It should take a few hours, but I don't plan on using the speed limits, I want to get there fast. So we won't be stopping very often." she said, looking in the back seat at the children.

"Do you hear that girls? I'm sorry but we need to get where we are going in a hurry so we can't stop a lot. So please don't drink too many juice boxes," I told the girls.

"We won't" they said.

"Are you alright? you have barely said anything since we left," I asked them.

"Yeah, we are just curious as to where we are going, and we don't want you to be worried, so we are trying to be good and quiet so you can relax, and focus," Sarah said.

"Thank you honey, but I am alright, you guys can talk, and enjoy the ride," I said with a smile, hoping it would ease the girl's minds. I didn't want them scared.

"Natasha, do you think we could make a quick stop? I really need some aspirin or something" I asked.

"Oh here, I have something that will help the pain, until we get you to the hospital," she said.

"Thank you, but I will not be going to the hospital, now or later, that is a paper trail right to us. I will be fine, I just need a bandage, and medicine and I will be fine," I said very sternly.

"No, Victoria you need a doctor, and I don't care what I have to do, when we get to that house, I am calling a doctor and having him come to the house and check you out," Natasha said just as sternly as I said to her.

"No, you won't, I will not risk anyone knowing our address, if I have to I will stop at the next hospital I see, so there is no way Dominic can find our new home," I demanded.

"Ok, thank you," Natasha said. "There is a hospital twenty minutes away, and we can stop for lunch and get you treated."

"I can't take the girls, I don't want them to have to wait around in a hospital waiting room," I said trying to make excuses not to go to the hospital.

"Victoria you said you would stop, I will take the girls to get food, and let them play at the park next to the hospital, and you and I can go to the hospital. Please Victoria, I just want to make sure you don't have a punctured lung or something," Natasha said in a pleading tone.

"Ok, I will but I am not going to stay long, I want in and out, and there will be no talk of Dominic, I will tell them I fell down the stairs," I ordered.

"Nicole, can you keep an eye on the girls while I run next door?" I asked.

"Of course, it will be fun, don't worry, just get yourself looked at," she said. She was years beyond her age. I wondered why she was so mature, I hoped that in time I would learn more about her. I kissed the girls, and told them to eat all their lunch and I would be right back.

As I sat there in the emergency room waiting area, I wondered if Dominic knew I would stop here, or if he set it up so I would have to go to the hospital.

"Natasha, I want to use a fake name, Alice Smith. It's common, and sounds real, and I will tell them I don't have insurance and just pay the bill"

"Ok, that should work, but please don't say my name out loud in here, I don't want to risk him finding us."

"Ok," she said. "I told you I will do anything for you, and I mean it," she replied.

"Alice" I heard, "Alice Smith," a woman called. I stood up and we went to the triage room, so she could do my vitals and then I would see the doctor. "Can you tell me how this happened, ma'am?" she asked.

"Yes, I was carrying laundry down the stairs, and I tripped over a toy, and fell," I told her.

"Ok, well your vitals sound good, and so do your lungs, but I think you have some broken ribs. Your cheek looks really bad, but it doesn't look very fresh, is that a previous stair falling wound?" she asked very suspiciously.

"No, I was in a car accident a few days ago, and the air bag went off, and that is what happened," I replied.

"Oh, well I would like to have the doctor take a look at it, if you don't mind," she said.

"Ok, but can we please make this quick, I have to go pick up my girls from a birthday party," I said. I couldn't believe how easy it was for me to come up with so many lies on the spot, I hated to lie, but I had no choice, I had to protect myself and my girls, I thought.

"Good Afternoon, Alice I am Dr. Ron, and I see you have been in a car accident and fell down some stairs," he said with a light smile.

"Yes, doctor" I said.

"Well you have four broken ribs, and your cheek bone is broken, but I am concerned with your eye socket, it is still very swollen. Do you mind if I take a better look at it?" he asked.

"Ok, but can we hurry?" I asked.

"Yes, I will hurry," he said as he began shining a light in my eye, and touching around it. "Ok, well it is definitely swollen, but I think it will be alright. I am going to give you some muscle relaxers, and an anti-inflammatory. The combination of the two will relax your muscles and take the swelling down, but you need to be careful. The muscle relaxer may make you tired, so no operating heavy machinery" he said with a laugh. "There is one more thing, I need to wrap your ribs, it is going to hurt, but it will keep them from, possibly puncturing a lung, so please brace yourself."

"Ok, but please I am in bit of a hurry," I said.

"Yes, ma'am, now hold still, this won't take long," he said as he began wrapping my ribs. "There, all done, here is your medicine and please take it easy," he warned.

"Ok, thank you," I said and grabbed my things and left.

The girls were having fun swinging and running, "Nicole, are they being good?" I asked as I went to her.

"Yes, they are angels, how are you? Is everything ok?" she asked.

"Yes, I have a few broken ribs, and my cheek is broken, but I will be fine," I said. "Girls, it's time to go," I called to them. They came running,.

"I like this place, it's fun," Stephanie said. Are there going to be swings and slides at our new home?" she asked.

"I don't know, but I think we can get some if there isn't," I said as I put them in the car.

"Natasha do you know how much longer it will be?" I asked.

"It should be about an hour and a half, I think," she said.

"That doesn't sound that bad," I said.

"Here take one of your pills, and relax," she said handing me a muscle relaxer.

"I don't know. What if it makes me sleepy?" I asked.

"Then you have an hour and a half to sleep, and relax" she said.

"Ok," I said taking the pill. "This is a really pretty area; Rhode Island is a beautiful state" I said.

"Yes it is, and the town we are going to is Riverside, it's less than an hour away from Providence, and it's very nice," she said. "There is even a farmers market, with fruit stands, and everything every morning, so we can have all the fresh fruit we want. We can even set up our own little stand if we want, and that way we can get to know the people," she said. The sound of that, made me very happy, I couldn't help but feel, happy and excited about our new venture.

"Hey, guess what Victoria? We are here, our house is at end of this road," Natasha said.

"Are we really? that didn't take long at all," I said. "The neighborhood looks so nice and peaceful."

"Yes, it's supposed to be the safest place in the world" she said.

"Really?" I asked.

"Ok, well maybe not the world, but it is ranked in the top ten" she said. "Victoria?"

"Yes Natasha. That is your house." she said, pointing to what looked to be a castle at the end of the road.

"What? that's not a house, it's a castle!" I said with amazement.

"I know, but it's the address, and look at the name," it said Strong.

"Oh my goodness, girls look at this, this is our new home," I said.

"Wow, are we princesses?" Stephanie asked.

"No, but it looks like we will be living like one," I said with a giggle.

We pulled up at the front door, and a little man with a butler's outfit stepped up and opened our door. "Good afternoon," he said as he bowed to us. "I am Nick, the butler, and you must be Victoria, Natasha, Sarah, Stephanie, and Nicole" he said.

"Yes we are," I said. "How did you know our names?" I asked as I stepped out of the car.

"Madame I have been with Joseph Strong, since he built this place, and so has everyone else here. We each have been told many times, that you guys would one day come here. We received letters and a life's wages when he passed away, and we were told to care for you and protect you when you came here. There is a letter for you two, from him, up in your suites. We are all so happy to have you here, we have heard so much about you, and we knew your mother," he said as he went to hug me. I stepped back unsure of what he was going to do. "I'm sorry miss, I don't mean to frighten you, and I know of your story, and I am very sorry you have been through that, but you are safe now, and we are all family here. Joseph insisted we call him by name, and he treated us as family, so please excuse us if we are a bit too friendly. We don't mean any harm, I assure you," he said offering a hug.

"Ok," I said smiling and hugged him.

"I hope you don't mind, but I sent most of the staff out for today, in anticipation for your arrival, I didn't want you guys to be overwhelmed by us when you got here, but there are still two maids, and a cook here who are going to be very happy. So again please excuse them," he said still smiling so sweetly.

As we went in the house, I thought I was dreaming. It looked like it was out of a fairy tale. It had high vaulted ceilings, crystal chandeliers, it was amazing. "Please allow us to show you to your suites," he said as two women in maids uniforms appeared at the top of the stairs. They both looked giddy, and excited. "Up there are two of your maids, Beth, and Sue. They have been here just as long as me, and they will be your personal maids to you and the girls," he said as we began walking up the stairs.

As we walked to our rooms, he was pointing and naming everything off, he seemed so proud of this place, and very protective of it. It was relaxing almost. Once in our rooms, there was everything we would need, clothes, shoes, under garments, even toiletries. Everything was an exact fit, and looked like we had lived here our whole lives. "How did you know what we like? and what sizes?" I asked.

"Oh, please don't be alarmed, but your grandfather had several people in your hometown giving him updates, and once he passed we continued, that's how we knew when you would be here. We wanted to go in and get you once we learned of the abuse, but we were bound to orders, not to interfere with your lives until you came to us. It was for your safety, so we obeyed, it was hard, but we had to. You see Dominic knew about this, but he knew he couldn't touch it without you, and even if you passed he couldn't touch it until you were aware of it. If you found out before you left him, he would kill you, and possibly the girls, and he would inherit it. Also, not to frighten you, but the whole town knows as well, and they will protect you as well. Your grandfather was loved by all, and he contributed to the town." This all seems like a dream, but could it be just the beginning of a new nightmare? Could this be part of Dominic's plan? I wondered.

As I started exploring the house, I noticed something familiar about the shoes on the floor by my door, they were Stephan's.

"Stephan?" I called "are you here?"

"Yes" I heard a voice say, as he stepped out of the room across from mine.

"How did you find this place?"

"I'm sorry Victoria, but I was one of the people who knew your grandfather. I didn't know everything, but my grandfather and yours were very close, and when they passed I received a letter with this address and instructions on keeping an eye on you. I know you may think I lied to you, but I didn't, I had to honor our grandfathers wishes for your safety and I'm glad I did,. You know how I feel about you, and all that is true, I promise you," he said.

"I understand, it's ok, honest" I said. "I understand. Nick has been explaining everything to me, and I am very confused, but how you feel about me, and your motives for everything, are not confusing me," I said and hugged him. I was truly happy to see him there. When he hugged me, I cried out from the pain in my ribs.

"What is it? Are you hurt?" he asked.

"There was an incident at the house this morning, I went down to make coffee and someone attacked me, but I'm ok. I went to the hospital in another town, and I have four broken ribs and a broken cheek bone, but I am ok," I said.

"I knew I shouldn't have left;" he began to say, and ranted about how he should've been there.

"Stop it," I demanded "you did the right thing so please don't blame yourself. I am still alive and hell, apparently I have a whole town and castle to protect me. So let's focus on the good things right now," I said.

"Mom look, there are toys, clothes; there is everything we want and need, how cool is this," Stephanie burst in and said.

"Stephanie sweetie, you don't have to call me mom here," I said. I didn't want her to think she needed to lie.

"I know, but I have always thought of you as mom, and I like calling you mom, can I still call you mom?"

"Yes, baby you can call me mom if you want, I have always felt you and your sister were my daughters and I like it when you call me mom," I told her.

"I love this place can we stay here forever please, please?" she begged.

"I think so, dear but right now I need to speak to Stephan, and Nick, so can you go play?" I asked her.

"Yes, mom, thank you," she said as she turned and ran out to play.

"Nick, can I talk to you for a moment?" I asked.

"Yes, Miss Victoria, what can I do for you?" he asked, eager to assist me.

"I am just a little worried, I just need a little reassurance that we are safe here, and even if it's just right now we are safe," I asked desperately hoping he would say yes.

"Miss. Victoria" he began to say.

"Nick please just call me Victoria," I interrupted.

"Ok, Victoria, you are safe, and if there comes a time when you are not safe, we as this house, and town, will protect you, I assure you" he said, very confidently.

"Thank you, Nick, it means the world to me, to be able to protect my girls, and to make them happy. So thank you," I said as I hugged him.

"You need not to thank me, ma'am, we are just doing what we have been doing for years. The only difference is that now we actually have you here, and there is something to bring joy to us all again."

"Still, thank you Nick. Is there anything we can do, or something?" I asked.

"No, just relax and unwind, we are planning a gourmet dinner tonight. If you would like to take a relaxing bath, and get dressed for dinner later, that would be nice. We are here to care for you, so please do whatever you like to relax and enjoy this wonderful day. Your heartaches and sorrows are over," he said.

As I walked with Stephan through the house, I was amazed by the family heritage on the walls, and I wondered if there was a picture of my mother, perhaps in her old room. "Stephan, do you know where my mother's room was?" I asked in hopes he would know.

"Actually Victoria I do. I remember when I came here once with grandfather. It was shortly after your grandfather heard of her death, and he was devastated. He told the staff to leave her room as it was, and no one was to go there again, he wanted it to remain as she had left it," he said as he lead the way to it. "If I remember correctly it should at the end of this hall. If my memory serves me well he remodeled these quarters in hopes when she returned with you and your sisters, she would live here. So he made her a home for you guys here in these quarters," he said.

"Really? Wow he really wanted her to return home, and regretted yelling at her," I said with a sense of sorrow for him.

"Here this I believe was her room," he said as we opened the door. "Here if you would like, I will leave you to get connected with her," he said.

"Yes, thank you, but could you possibly check on the girls, and send Natasha up here? I think she would like this too," I asked.

"Of course, I will see what she is up to, and tell her to come up here."

"Thank you," I said.

As I stood there in her room, I tried to picture her as she was the last day she was in this room, and what she must have felt. I began looking through things, trying to get a feel for her, I wondered if she had a diary. As I was searching for something that would tell me more, I noticed something tucked under the corner of her mattress. As I pulled it out I noticed it was a diary. Should I read it? I opened it to the last entry.

I told my father I was with child, and I tried to explain what happened, but he wouldn't listen, I knew he wouldn't. How can I explain that it wasn't my fault, but I had decided to keep them, I didn't even get a chance to tell him I was having twins, and they are girls. I was hoping he wouldn't freak out on me, after all I am 25 years old, and it wasn't my fault. I know what I have to do, but it's going to be hard to leave everything I have ever known, but if I don't he will never understand, and Luke may find me, and if he finds me he will kill me, and I can't risk my girls.

That was it, what could my mother be talking about, why was she so scared of Luke? Who was Luke? I wondered. I must have zoned out, because I never heard Natasha enter the room, and she startled me when I felt her hand on my shoulder. "Victoria, are you ok?" she asked as I jumped. "I said your name three times, and you didn't answer," she said.

"Oh, I'm sorry. Look I found Mom's diary, and guess what? We are twins, but she was scared of a man named Luke, and she kept saying it wasn't her fault," I told her.

"Wow, I wonder what she was talking about? Did something happen to her before?" she asked concerned.

" I don't know I only read the last entry, I wanted to know what she felt the last day she was here," I said.

"Well, read from before that, and see what she is talking about," Natasha demanded.

"I will but give me a second, patience, Natasha patience," I said.

"Hey, Victoria, Natasha are you still up here?" we heard Stephan say as he was coming down the hall.

"Well, I guess we will find out later, I don't want anyone to know, until we actually know what she was talking about," I told Natasha.

"Yes, we are in here," Natasha called to Stephan.

"Oh hey, did I interrupt you guys? If so I'm sorry, but Luke sent me up to tell you that dinner is in half an hour, so if you want to start getting ready that would be great," he said.

"Ok, do they dress for dinner here, or something?" I asked.

"Oh yeah, I forgot to tell you, they do it similar to how you did it before, but they are used to lunch being formal for regular dinners, it's how your grandfather has done it ever since he was a child. The staff would like to keep it that way, if it's alright with you Victoria," he said, hoping I would ok it.

"Of course, I don't mind, I think it's very important to have family dinners, and if we have to make time to dress for it, then so be it," I said with a smile. "Well shall we go get dressed and see to the children?" I asked giving Natasha a glance.

"Oh, yes that is a marvelous idea," she gasped and rushed out to check the girls.

"Did I miss something? What are you and Natasha plotting?" Stephan asked skeptically. "I remember you two always ganging up on me as a child, so I know the secret glances, what's up?" Stephan asked again.

"Oh, nothing we were just talking about everything, I mean it's weird we are sisters now, and we grew up together acting like sisters, but now we really are. That's a lot to digest, and we were just talking," I told him, I hate lying to him, but I couldn't tell him yet, I mean after all I just found out about my sisters and well one of us has or had a twin. I want to deal with one thing at a time, especially when it comes to the girls, I thought to myself, as I walked out of mother's room, behind Stephan.

"Stephan, what should I wear tonight? There are so many wonderful dresses in here, but I don't want to over dress or under dress," I asked a little confused.

"Well, you would never look under dressed; you are always the most beautiful woman in any room, or place," he said with a hint of love in his eyes. It was like there was a weight lifted off of him since he told me that he knew about my grandfather, like he was complete now. I liked seeing him like this, and it was nice. “Why don’t you wear this black one, it’s nice casual, but semi formal, and besides black always is the best choice, you look like a goddess in a black dress,” he said.

“Ok, I am going to take a shower and get dressed, thank you for helping me pick one. Will you check on the girls and make sure they are listening to Nicole, and Natasha?” I asked as I walked in the bathroom.

“Yeah right on it,” he said as he walked out.

I began to undress, and realized there weren’t any towels in the bathroom, so I walked back into the bedroom, and Stephan walked back in, I froze. I was standing there completely naked. “Oh, I’m sorry” he said and immediately turned his head, then immediately turned back looking directly at the bruises on my body, my ribs, and the scar on the inside of my thigh. “Victoria, please tell me that those aren’t all from him,” he said. I could see the pain in his eyes.

“Some are,” I said as I grabbed the blanket from the chair to cover my exposed body.

“Victoria, why didn’t you tell me he was beating you like this? I mean I knew he was wicked, but I thought the night you left was the first time he laid a hand on you," he said. "I should've seen it, I am so sorry Victoria," he said, I could see he wanted to cry, and kill Dominic.

"It's fine Stephan, I am fine, so please let it go," I said sternly.

"Ok, but one question, what is that scar on your thigh from?" he asked.

"It's from Dominic, he did it shortly after we married. I found out I was pregnant and I was sick, and very tired, so I didn't feel like satisfying his needs the way a wife should. He got upset and he pushed me and I fell into the crystal vase and broke the mirror, and that made him madder. When I tried to defend myself, he became even more angry, and he sort of threw me and when I fell a piece of the broken mirror went into my thigh, and I lost the baby," as I told him that the tears began to stream down my cheeks.

"I'm sorry Victoria," he said as he grabbed me and held me so tight, it hurt, but it felt wonderful to be in caring arms.

"Stephan it is ok. I left him, and I am never going back, that part of my life is over, so let's not dwell on that part of the past," I asked him.

“You’re right, let’s focus on the present, and keeping you guy’s safe,” he said brushing the hair off my face. “Now go take that shower, and I will meet you downstairs,” he said and left the room.

The shower felt wonderful, and the dress Stephan picked out was beautiful, and it flowed evenly as I walked. As I walked down the stairs, it felt almost magical. There was something about this house, and this town. There was something magical here. The halls lit up whenever someone entered them, the lights on the walls glowed vigorously. It all seemed so odd to me, it’s almost as if Grandfather was watching, even though I had never met him, I could feel his presence everywhere.

“There you are Victoria, I was wondering if everything was ok, or if you got lost,” Natasha said with a giggle.

“Sorry, I kind of got caught up with all the history in the halls, and had to stop and look at each picture,” I said, hoping it would be satisfying.

“It happens all the time,” Nick said with a smile. “I hope you like chicken, the chef has prepared a family recipe, and I hope you enjoy it,” Nick said as he brought out our plates.

"Excuse me Nick, but aren't you and the rest of the staff going to join us tonight?" I asked.

"Oh, no ma'am, it is your dinner, we will eat in the kitchen," he said.

"Well if you don't mind, I would like you and the rest to join us at the table, this is such huge table, and there is plenty of food, please join us," I insisted.

"Yes, ma'am" he said as he went to get the staff. I had always wanted our staff back home to eat with us, after all they prepared and served it, but Dominic always said they were beneath us and didn't deserve to eat with us.

"Thank you ma'am" Nick and the others said as they came to sit at the table, they all looked a little uncomfortable.

"I hope you guys don't mind but from now on, I would like us all to eat together, when it is just us," I said.

"Thank you very much ma'am, but we couldn't possibly," he started to say.

"Nonsense, you will join us at dinner, when it's just us, I insist," I said.

"Well thank you ma'am," they said.

"Dinner was delicious, and everything was wonderful," I said.

"Yes it was," Stephan agreed.

"Victoria, if you don't mind, I would like to take the girls up and get them ready for bed?" Nicole asked.

"Oh no, Miss. Nicole, please allow me to see to the children," Beth said.

"Excuse me, I will see to the children," Nicole demanded.

"Nicole, sweetie she didn't mean to offend you, she was just doing her job, remember you are not staff anymore, you're a member of the family," I said to her.

"Beth, I'm sorry. I guess I'm not used to having family, you see I was their nanny, and Victoria was always good to me, and treated me as a daughter, but to me it's my honor to see to the children," Nicole explained.

"It's alright, Miss Nicole, please allow me, but if you would like you may come up with me, and make sure I do it right," Beth offered.

"Thank you, Beth I will come up but I have no doubt in your abilities to care for the girls," Nicole said.

"Thank you both very much, I will be up in a few minutes to say good night to them," I said.

"Good night, we love you," the girls came up and said as they hugged me.

"Victoria, how are you feeling, are your ribs alright?" Natasha asked.

"I am good, my ribs are a little tender but I will be fine," I said not sure why Natasha asked that in front of everyone.

"Would anyone care for a glass of wine or something?" Nick asked.

"Actually, I think I would like a glass of white wine," I said. "Thank you, Nick."

"If you would like to retreat to the family room I would be happy to have drinks waiting for you," he said.

"Thank you," Stephan said as he stood up.

"I think I will go up and say good night to the girls and see if Nicole would like anything," I said.

"Sarah, Stephanie, and Nicole" I said as I entered the room. "Are you guys ok, and ready for bed?" I asked.

"Yes, we are. Beth is very nice, she offered to bring in a bed for Nicole," Sarah said.

"Nicole, do you want to sleep in here? Because there is a door to this room in your room, so you will still be near them if you want. I would rather you sleep in your own room, so the girls get used to sleeping in their own rooms again," I said hoping Nicole would understand.

"Yes, I think that would be best girls, we have a new home now, and you are safe, so you will be fine in here. If you need me, just go through that door, or the door over there goes to Victoria's room," Nicole said with a soft smile trying to reassure the girls.

"Ok, we will, we like this place. Do you think tomorrow we can go outside and play on all those toys out there?" Stephanie asked.

"Maybe, if it's nice out," I said. "Good night girls. Sleep tight, if you need me, come get me, I love you," I said as I kissed them good night.

"How are the girls?" Natasha asked as I entered the family room.

"They are good, they can't wait to play outside on all those toys," I told her with a giggle.

"Victoria, is it alright if I take a bath and get ready for bed?" Nicole came in and asked.

"Of course dear, please relax, and unwind, and you don't need to ask," I said.

"Thank you," she said as she walked out.

"Why does she feel she has to ask to do anything?" Stephan asked.

"I think it is because of Dominic, she has been with us since we got the girls, so she is still very timid, but she is slowly opening up more," I said.

"Victoria, I think we should discuss what we found today," Natasha said abruptly.

"Natasha I thought we decided to wait until we found out more," I said sharply.

"What are you two talking about?" Stephan interrupted.

"Fine, we are talking about our mother's diary. We found it today and we read the last entry, it was the day she left this place," I said.

"We were about to read more, but you came in and we couldn't," Natasha said to Stephan.

"Ok, well what did you find out?" he asked curiously.

"That one of us is a twin, we aren't sure who yet, and she kept saying it wasn't her fault, but she couldn't stay here because Luke would kill her," I told him.

"Wow! That is weird. Who is Luke?"

"We aren't sure yet," I said.

"Where is the diary?" Stephan asked.

"Oh, it's right here," Natasha said, pulling it out.

"Well let's read from before," Stephan said impatiently.

"Ok, we will, but first close the door, just to be safe," I said. I started reading; I believe it was a few months prior.

"Wow, today was amazing, I met this guy Luke, he is wonderful, he asked me to go out with him this weekend, I hope my father lets me. He has the most beautiful green eyes, and dark, almost black hair. I guess he is from out of town, but is thinking of moving here. I must figure out what to wear, should I wear a dress or a skirt? I am so excited, I can't wait."

"What else does it say? Stephan asked.

"Nothing. That's all it says for that day and none of the entries have a date on them, that is so weird," I said.

"Read after that, go to their date, and see what happened," Natasha demanded.

"Ok, hold on let me find it," I said. "Here it is."

"Well Luke turned out to be worse than I ever imagined. I think he is after my father's money, but I can't be sure. The date started out nice, we went to dinner, then for a walk through the park. And he asked me to go for a walk down by the river, so we did but it turned out very bad. He kissed me, that was sweet at first, but then he kept trying to lay me down, and I told him I couldn't, and I didn't want to rush things. He became upset, and slapped me, and started calling me names. I tried to run but he was too strong, and grabbed me, and I fell. Then he pinned me down, and made me do it, I kept tell him to stop, but he didn't listen. When he was done, I just laid there unable to move, my body hurt so bad, and he left me there, and threatened to kill me if I told. I want to tell my father, but I can't, he would be so mad."

"Oh, my goodness can you believe that?" Natasha said.

"Wow, what happened after that?" Stephan asked.

"Ok, I will read more to see what else happened."

"It's been a month or so since that night, things are getting better, but I have been feeling very tired, and sick, I hope I'm not pregnant. I think I am going to go to the doctor, and find out for sure. I am very scared, what am I going to tell my father if I am? Last time I told my father I was pregnant, and he freaked, but I was only 16, and I couldn't care for a child. I wish things would've happened differently, but I couldn't help the slippery roads, and I went in the ditch. I wish Violet would've made it, but maybe that was for the best. I will never forget the look on my father's face when he told me I lost the baby, it was almost eerie."

"So does that mean, you and Natasha are twins?" Stephan asked in confusion.

"Did grandfather lie to our mother, and tell her Violet died? When he really sent her away to live in the orphanage? I am very confused now," I said. "I'm not sure what is going on, but I don't want to know right now, so much has happened and it seems like there are more skeletons in these closets, let's just keep them closed for now," I said closing the diary, and putting it away.

"More wine anyone?" Nick came in and asked.

"Yes, please" I said. "Thank you Nick, you are very kind" I said as I took a sip of my wine, trying to relax more and not think about anything we had just found out.

"So, Natasha what are you going to do now?" Stephan asked.

"Are you going to see more of Luke?" I asked cautiously.

"Actually I am meeting Luke tomorrow, a few towns over, and I might stay the night if it is ok with you Victoria?" she asked.

"Of course Natasha if you want to stay with Luke tomorrow night," I said shocked that she would ask my permission.

"Stephan what are you going to do now?" I asked.

"Well, if you two don't mind I was thinking of buying a house here in town, so I could still keep an eye on you guys," he said.

"Well, I understand you wanting to be near us, but why buy a house, there are many rooms. I mean hell there are several quarters in this place, you would have your own privacy, so please stay here, I insist," I said. The thought of him not being in the next room, scared me half to death.

"Well, I wouldn't want to impose," he said, "but if you insist" he said with a smile.

"Good, I insist."

"That deserves a toast" Natasha said, "To new beginnings, and to the ending of a nightmare," Natasha said raising her glass. I nodded, but for some reason, I felt that the ending of the nightmare was truly the beginning of something much worse.

"Well you guys I am going to head up stairs for bed. I am going to check on the girls, I said as I stood up."

"Good night Victoria," Natasha said.

"I will be up in a minute, to say good night," Stephan said.

"Ok, thank you," I said.

The girls were asleep, so was Nicole. I couldn't wait to crawl in bed; it had been a very long day. As I began to undress, I heard a light knock on the door, "just a minute" I called. I quickly put on my night gown. "Come in."

"I didn't mean to interrupt you," Stephan said as he came in.

"You didn't" I said with a smile.

"You look exhausted, are you feeling ok?" he asked.

"Yeah I am just a little tired, it has been a long few days, and I think it has all just caught up to me," I said.

"Well why don't you get some sleep, and I will see you in the morning?" he said.

"Thank you, Stephan you have been truly wonderful, and I appreciate it, I really do," I said as I set my hand on his arm.

"I would do anything for you Victoria, and I hope you know that," he said leaning in to kiss my forehead.

"Thank you, have a good night's sleep,"

"Good night Stephan," I said kissing his hand. How I longed to be with him, but I couldn't risk it, I thought to myself.

"Good night Victoria" he said as he walked out.

I awoke abruptly to a very loud scream; I leaped out of bed and rushed to the girls. "What happened, are you ok?" I yelled as I entered the room. Stephan and Natasha came rushing in shortly after me.

"What is it? What happened?" they asked at the same time.

"I'm sorry to frighten all of you, but I thought I saw someone outside my window," Sarah said, very scared like.

"It's ok, baby, I'm here," I said hugging her.

"Stephan will you please go check it out?" I asked, knowing he would.

"Of course, I was already on my way, don't worry Sarah, I will make sure it is ok," he said as he left the room. As I sat there hugging her, I realized the girls were more frightened than I had thought. Moments later, Stephan returned with Nick.

"Well, was anyone out there?" I asked in a sharp tone.

"I will let Nick explain," Stephan said with a smile.

"Ok, I am very sorry you are scared Miss Sarah, but yes there was a man outside your window. He is our gardener, and he was cleaning the gutters, he does it every week, and I hadn't told him yet that you guys were here. I promise he means no harm," Nick said with complete sympathy for frightening the child.

"It's alright Nick, I understand, do you understand Sarah? Are you ok now?" I asked.

"Yeah, I'm ok, can we have breakfast now, I am really hungry," she said. We all laughed, children are so innocent, it's a wonderful thing, I thought.

"I will take you girls downstairs and get your breakfast," Nick said to the girls.

"Hey Victoria are you ok?' Stephan asked.

"Yes I am, I was very concerned when I heard the scream," I said. "Now, Stephan are you sure it was just a gardener out there," I asked.

"Yes, I am, Victoria that's one thing you don't need to worry about here, people are honestly here to protect you," he said reassuring me that it was ok.

"Victoria, you have to trust some people to be safe, and happy," Natasha warned.

"I know. I am just being cautious" I said.

"Ok, well why don't we go get ready for breakfast and we can start figuring out what to do?" Natasha said.

"Ok, I will be down in a minute or so," I said. "I just need a minute to get dressed and go down stairs."

"Ok, we will meet you down there," Natasha said.

I stood there looking at the window, and I noticed there were no gutters outside this window, so I opened it and looked out further, and I saw there was a gutter laying on the ground. Perhaps he was just cleaning it and it fell when he heard the scream, yes that is what happened I said to myself, more to convince me that it was all ok. I went and dressed for breakfast.

“Well that was quite the excitement” I said as I entered and sat at the table.

“Yes it was” Stephan agreed with a laugh.

“Mmm, something smells wonderful, Nick, what is it?” I asked.

“Oh, it is eggs Benedict; it is the chef's favorite thing to make for breakfast. It has all the nutrition, and taste you need for the perfect start of the day,” he said standing a little taller, more proud.

“Well it sounds wonderful,” Natasha said.

“Mom, can we have cereal instead of this?” Stephanie asked.

“Yes, honey you two can have cereal,” I said as I went to stand up to go to the kitchen.

“Oh no ma'am, I will get the little misses some cereal,” Nick said.

“Are you sure? I don't mind” I said.

“Of course ma'am, but please allow me to do it,” he said.

“Ok, thank you Nick, girls what do you say to Nick?” I asked looking at them.

"Oh yes, Thank you very much Nick," both girls said.

"Nicole, are you ok?" I asked.

"Yes, I am just tired this morning, I didn't sleep well last night, there are a lot of noises in this house, and I guess it is going to take me a while to get used to them," she said.

"Nicole if you need anything please let me know, I will do anything to make you comfortable, so please honey if you need anything let me know," I told her.

"Ok, thank you ma'am," she said.

"Nicole would you like to come with me today?" Natasha asked.

"Where are you going?" she asked.

"I am going to go shopping in Providence today, and then I am getting a room at the Plaza. If you would like to come, I would love it, I will even get you a room at the plaza, and you can have everything you want," Natasha asked hoping she would say yes.

"Oh, I don't know Miss. Natasha I couldn't leave Victoria and the girls," she said.

"Oh honey, if you want to go with Natasha you can, I think it would be good for you to go out, and have a little fun, but if you don't want to stay there, I would be happy to come up and get you tonight," I offered.

"Well, I don't want you to have to drive to get me," she said. She was always thinking of everyone else's need before her own, I thought.

"Nicole, if I remember correctly, your birthday is coming up, so why don't you go with Natasha and you two can go shopping, and get some news clothes, maybe even a new dress to wear the night of your party?" I said.

"Ma'am, a party for me?" she said.

"Yes, honey, you are going to be 16 aren't you?" I asked.

"Yes, I am but how did you know that?" she said.

"Honey, I have always thought of you as my daughter, and do you remember every year on holidays and birthdays you got a present under your bed?" I said.

"Yes, I do remember. I thought it was from the staff," she said.

"I know. I always told them to make you think it was from them so Dominic wouldn't find out," I told her. I could see the tears burning in her eyelids. "Nicole it is your call if you want, you can," I said.

"I think I will," she said, "but I will stay the night, it might be nice," she continued.

"Good, I'm very happy to hear that. Nicole, have fun," I said.

"Mom, we are all done eating, can we go play?" Sarah asked.

"Yes, but be careful, and make sure Beth knows you are outside, and ask her if she would go outside with you," I said.

"Ok, we will. Thank you." they yelled as they went running out to play.

"Nicole, once we are done with breakfast, we should go up and get ready to go, we need to leave soon," Natasha said.

"Ok, I will go up and get ready, right now" Nicole said with excitement dripping from her words.

"Natasha that was very kind of you to include Nicole, she needs to have fun," I said.

"Of course Victoria, I am curious how she will be, when she can let loose, and not worry," Natasha said.

"Please keep an eye on her," I warned. "I don't want anything to happen to her," I said.

"Relax Victoria, I will protect her," she said as she went to go get ready.

"Stephan do you think this is a good idea, for Nicole to go with Natasha?" I asked.

"Yes, I think it will be good for her to get away, maybe then she will start to accept that she is family, not staff," he said.

"You're right, I'm sorry," I said.

"Hey why don't we go into town today, and get some things to redecorate a little? After all this is your new place, and I need some things too," he said.

"Oh yeah, I forgot to tell you yesterday, I sold my house. I made it known that I sold my business, and relocated to Canada for a new business, so you don't need to worry about Dominic finding us. He thinks I'm in Canada, and so he will probably think you are there too," he said.

"That is wonderful, but did you buy a business in Canada?" I asked.

"Yes, actually I did, but I have someone in control, and all I need to do is communicate through the internet," he said happily.

"That is wonderful Stephan, let's do it, let's go to town and get some stuff to redecorate this place," I said.

"Maybe we can have Beth watch the girls, and we can grab lunch or something," I offered. His face lit right up when I said that.

"That is a wonderful idea, Victoria," he said leaning in to kiss my hand.

"Ok, I will ask Beth, and get ready," I said as I left the room.

"Beth, is it ok, if Stephan and I go into town today, and you could watch the girls?" I said cautiously.

"Of course madam, please go and have a good time, there are many little shops in town, and I would be honored to watch the girls. Thank you Miss Victoria," Beth said hugging me.

"Thank you very much," I said as I went to tell the girls. "Sarah, Stephanie come here please," I called to them.

"What is it?" they said running up to me.

"Stephan and I are going to town for a while, and Beth is in charge so please listen and be good," I said to them.

"Ok, we will, can we go back and play now?" Stephanie said with little puppy dog eyes.

"Yes, go play but be careful."

"We will" they called as they ran back to play.

"Thank you Beth, if you need anything please call me on Stephan's cell," I said as I turned to go get ready.

"Stephan are you ready?" I asked as I entered his bedroom.

"Yes, almost" he said coming out of the bathroom with his shirt off.

"I'm sorry, I didn't mean to interrupt" I said as I turned my head. I couldn't believe how defined his stomach and chest were, and so tanned. I couldn't help but want to look.

"Oh you didn't, I just have to throw on a shirt and I am ready," he said grabbing a t-shirt from the drawer.

"Wow, you look very different in rugged jeans and a t-shirt, I am used to you wearing a suit jacket and slacks, but you look good," I said. I too was wearing very casual clothing, and it felt great to have on my ripped up jeans and a tank top. Dominic would get mad if I tried to wear anything that wasn't formal.

"Well you look good yourself Victoria, I like the holy pants," he said with a smile. "Shall we Miss Victoria?" he said holding out his arm for me to take.

"We shall," I said with a laugh. I felt like a little girl again, it was nice. No worrying, no running, just hanging out.

As we walked through town, and into stores, I realized how perfect this town was. No one questioned me, or was looking at me any differently than they did the regular townspeople. “Oh Stephan look at that shirt, it’s perfect for Nick, I am going to get it for him,” I said with excitement.

“You are too funny Victoria, you love buying for people, and spoiling the staff,” he said with a laugh.

“I can’t help it, they do so much for us, and Dominic would never let me buy them gifts or even treat them nicely, and now I can, so I will,” I said smiling. I didn’t realize that the smile hadn’t left my face all day, and Stephan noticed it.

“I like seeing you smile Victoria, it’s been so long since I’ve seen that beautiful natural smile on your face, and today I see it nonstop,” he said smiling.

“Today is the beginning of the future, I am going to stop worrying about everything, and start living. I spent too much time scared, and so did the girls. I know it’s not over with Dominic, but I will stand up to him, and protect the ones I love,” I declared proudly to him.

“Good, I’m proud of you Victoria, now let’s enjoy the day,” he said leading the way to another store. We stopped for lunch at this cute little deli, the food was wonderful.

"Stephan, we should be heading home soon," I said. I heard the phone ring, "Stephan your phone, it could be Beth," I said with panic in my voice.

"Hello," he said answering it, "it's for you Victoria, it's Beth."

"Beth what is it?" I asked answering the phone.

"Ma'am I am very sorry, but Stephanie fell off the play set, and I think her arm might be broken," she said. I could hear the sorrow in her voice.

"Ok I will be right there," I said and hung up. "We need to go. Stephanie fell and might have broken her arm," I said frantically.

"Ok, relax, it's ok, we will take her to the hospital," he said trying to calm me down.

"Just hurry and get me to her please," I asked with fear dripping from my words.

"Ok, I will" he said as he put the car in gear, and sped away.

The car wasn't even completely stopped, and I was opening the door, and leaping out to get my baby girl. "Stephanie, are you ok?" I asked as I reached her.

"Yes, but my arm really hurts," she said holding up her arm to show me. It was very swollen.

"I think we better take you in to get checked," I said calmly trying not to frighten her.

"Ok, I'm sorry Mom, I didn't mean to," she said.

"Oh, baby it's not your fault, accidents happen and you are just a child, I understand, I just want to make sure you're alright, ok baby?" I said carrying her to the car, where Stephan was waiting.

"Ok, Mommy, thank you," she said hugging me.

We pulled up to the emergency room entrance. I got out still holding Stephanie. As I went up to the desk, there was a short little round woman sitting in a chair eating potato chips, "excuse me ma'am, I need to see a doctor, my daughter fell, and I think she has a broken arm," I said with tears starting to fall.

"Ok, go through that doorway, and wait for the doctor to come in," she said, pointing to the door that had triage painted on it in red blocky writing.

"Ok," I said as I walked into the room. Moments later the doctor came.

"What seems to be the problem?" he asked looking at Stephanie. He was about average height, very slim but looked very young. "I am Dr. Mills, what happened to your arm little miss?" he said looking at Stephanie with a very soft look in his eyes.

"I fell" she said.

"Ok, well can I look at you arm?" he asked her.

"Yes, but be careful it really hurts," she said.

"I will be careful, I promise," he said. "Well, ma'am it is definitely broken, and I am going to need to fit her for a cast. If you don't mind I need to take her in back, but you are welcome to go out in the waiting room, and wait, it should only take about twenty minutes," he said.

"Like hell, I am her mother, and I will be going with her," I said very sternly.

"Miss, I understand you want to be with her, but it is easier to do it without you, parents tend to ask questions, and make it take longer, so if you want this to go fast, please wait here," he said in a very aggravated tone.

"Fine, I will wait here, but you better take good care of her," I threatened.

"I will I promise," he said in a much softer tone.

As I waited in the waiting area I noticed the nurses, who seemed to be watching too closely to what I was doing. "Stephan, why does that woman at the nurse's station keep watching me so closely?" I asked.

"I am not sure, but she is very intent on what you are doing," he said.

"Excuse me a minute," I said to Stephan, as I got up to walk over to her.

"Wait Victoria, don't," Stephan warned.

"Why not, I am just going to ask her why she is watching me," I said in a defiant tone.

"If you do that, then you are bringing more attention to yourself, and if you act like just another concerned parent chances are she isn't going to be a problem," he said.

"Ok, I guess you are right, I probably shouldn't draw more attention than other parents in here," I said sitting back down in my seat. He was right, I need to relax, I thought.

"Victoria Strong," I heard a man call.

"Yes, that is me" I said standing up to go to him. I had to use Strong as my last name, so it wouldn't get back to Dominic.

"Stephanie is fine, she is a little groggy because we gave her a mild sedative to calm her while we fitted her for a cast," he said. "Also if you would just sign some papers, we can get you guys out of here," he continued.

"Ok, what do I need to sign?" I asked.

"Here Victoria you take care of the paperwork, and I will go get Stephanie," Stephan offered, to speed the process up.

"Yeah, please go get her," I asked.

"Victoria, please sign this line, and on the next two pages sign the highlighted areas," he asked. I did so, but without even thinking, I didn't read them, I just signed my name.

"Are we all set now?" Stephan asked as he came out carrying Stephanie, who had a pink flowered cast on her arm.

"Yes, we are, now let's get you home," I said smiling so she would be relaxed. The whole way home she was very quiet, I think the medicine was making her sleepy. "Stephan is she ok?" I asked just for reassurance.

"Yes, she is, she just needs to go home and get some rest," he said calmly. As we pulled into the driveway, I noticed a strange vehicle, it was Luke's.

"What is he doing here?" I snapped.

"I'm not sure," Stephan said with confusion.

I went straight into the house, and there he was sitting on the sofa in the family room. "What are you doing here, and where are Natasha and Nicole?" I asked.

“Oh, them, they aren’t here,” he said in a very strange tone.

“Ok, why are you here?” I snapped unsure of what was happening.

"There was an accident,” he said. Those words hit me like a brick.

“What do you mean accident?” I cried.

“You will see, you will see,” he said.

“What are you talking about?” I screamed, “Where’s my sister, and Nicole? If you hurt them I will kill you,” I screamed.

“Hey, what happened?” Stephan came rushing in and asked.

“He said there was an accident,” I cried, “but he won’t tell me anything else,” I said with tears streaming down my cheeks.

Stephan, grabbed him and held him up to the wall by his throat, and said “I am only asking you this once, where are Nicole and Natasha? and you better think really hard, before you lie, because at this angle I can snap your neck with a slight switch of my wrist, so where are they?”

“Ok, ok, I will tell you, they are at the plaza in Providence, and I was coming here to get Victoria,” he said still gasping for air.

"Why were you coming to get Victoria?" Stephan asked still holding him by the throat.

"I was coming to get her so I could take her to Natasha. Something has happened to them, they were in an accident," he said.

"Why were you acting so strange?" I asked.

"I don't know, I'm scared I guess, because I know you don't trust me, and then your boyfriend comes in and chokes me," he said.

"Ok, well let's go," I said. "I need to go to them," I cried.

"Stephan, will you follow us in your car," Luke asked.

"Why do I need to follow? I will ride with you," he said.

"If you ride with us there won't be room for all of us, plus Natasha and Nicole," he said.

"Ok, but don't try anything stupid," Stephan warned. I was very unsure of this discussion, but if something was wrong with those two, I didn't have time to wait and see what happened.

"Beth?" I called.

"Yes, madam?"

"I have to go to Providence. Can you take care of the girls?" I asked.

"Of course miss, go please, be careful," she said with suspicion in her eyes. I nodded, and left.

"It is only about an hour drive," Luke said. The roads were unfamiliar and I had a very bad feeling. "Victoria there is a soda if you would like something to drink, it's unopened," he said offering me a can of soda.

"No, thank you," I said. I was still very nervous. "Is Stephan still behind us?" I asked as I looked in the rear view mirror.

"Yes he is, that's him," he said referring to the headlights.

"Are we almost there?" I asked trying not to sound inpatient.

"Not quite, but we are getting closer," he said. We are in the middle of nowhere I thought to myself, why would he be taking all of these back roads, and deer trails?

"What's that up there?" I said as I saw a man waving us down.

"Let's find out," he said.

"Can I help you sir?" Luke said as he pulled over to see what was going on.

"Yes it's my brother he has been out cold for awhile, and he won't wake up," the man said looking directly at Luke.

Moments later Stephan, came walking up slowly, "what seems to be the trouble?" he asked.

"It's my brother," the man said telling Stephan the same thing he told us. Stephan walked over to the man on the ground, and began looking at him. Luke whipped the car in reverse, and went flying backwards.

"What are you doing?" I screamed. I looked ahead to see if Stephan was ok, and just as I did I saw the man on the ground stand up, and hit Stephan with something. "Oh my goodness, you are working for Dominic aren't you?" I screamed. "Let me out," I said as I began slapping him, and trying to open the car door. He grabbed my hands, and hit me knocking me against the window. "You have to stop, I need to make sure Stephan is ok," I cried.

"Look, Stephan is fine, and he will be fine, as long as you do what you are told," he screamed.

"Ok, I will, what do I have to do?"

"That's not up to me, that's up to Dominic. He has been very worried about you since you ran away. You know he loves you very much," Luke said.

"Like hell he does, Dominic is a monster, I am nothing more than a possession to him," I demanded. "You have no clue, what Dominic is like, he is very powerful, and just as evil, so you don't have any right to tell me about him," I said anger and resentment dripping off ever word.

"I don't give a shit, what he has said or done to you, all I know is I am being paid a shit load of cash to date Natasha and bring you to him. So why don't you just sit down, and shut the hell up," he ordered.

It was at that moment that I knew I couldn't let him bring me back to Dominic, but how was I going to escape? How I could get away from him, and get to Natasha and Nicole? "Luke, was there really an accident or was that a cover up to get me to come with you?" I asked.

"Actually, no I haven't seen Natasha since that day at the other house, when you got your ribs broken. That was me," he confessed.

"What? that was you, why, why would you do that to me, you don't even know me?" I said in complete shock. "What kind of monster are you, to attack a woman with her children in the house, a woman who has been beaten hundreds of times by her husband, and you just sneak in and attack her, you are a monster," I cried.

"Shut up, you stupid, stupid woman," he yelled as he swung his arm to hit me, but I moved knowing he would hit the window and get distracted. "You Bitch" he yelled, pulling the car to the side of the road.

"What are you going to do?" I asked pretending to be terrified. "please don't" I said, "please I am begging you," I cried.

"Get out now," he ordered.

"No, please don't," I kept repeating to myself knowing it would make him mad enough, forget things, little things. "Please no, please don't" I screamed getting more and more hysterical.

"Shut up, shut up, shut up," he repeated each time getting louder. Then he finally grabbed the door handle and opened his door, and came around to the other side. I jumped in the driver's seat, slamming the door, and locking them.

"Hey, get out right now, I am going to kill you bitch," he screamed from outside the locked vehicle.

"Hey, guess what Luke?" I asked.

"What?" he yelled.

"Go to hell," I yelled as I put it in reverse and then floored forward knowing I was going to hit him, and once I hit him, I kept going. I had to protect the ones I loved.

I drove back to where Stephan was, and sure enough he was laying on the ground, out cold. I got out and ran to him. "Stephan are you ok?" I cried hoping he would be. He didn't wake up. "Oh Stephan please wake up," I cried again. "I can't live without you, I love you, please wake up so I can tell you I love you please, please wake," I laid my head on him sobbing, I didn't want him to die, he has been the love of my life since we were kids, and I couldn't lose him. "Please Stephan wake up," I said again.

"Vic, Victoria is that you?" I heard him say in a groggy tone.

"Yes, it is" I screamed with joy, "you're not dead, I love you Stephan, I love you, and I am so sorry I let this happen to you," I said still hanging on to him very tightly.

"Hey, it's ok I am fine, just a small bump on the head," he said.

"We have to get home, the girls could be in danger," I said realizing that this wasn't over yet.

"Let's go" he said, grabbing my hand and running to the car.

"We are almost there Victoria, but when we get there remember I am here, and so is Nick, we will protect you," he said holding my hand.

"Ok, but please hurry, I can't lose them" I said squeezing his hand a little harder.

"It is going to be ok, I promise" he said.

"Thank you Stephan, you mean the world to me, what would I do without you?" I asked not really expecting an answer.

"Victoria, you are a very strong woman, and you would be fine without me, you just wouldn't have anyone to remind you of that," he said smiling softly at me. "We are almost there, just a few more miles and we are there," Stephan said.

"Ok," I said as I began looking through the glove box, and things in the car.

"What are you looking for?" Stephan asked.

"A gun or something," I said.

"Ok, but be careful," he said.

"We are here, now when we go inside, go through the main door, I am going to sneak in through a window or something, so they don't expect me," Stephan advised.

"Ok," I said getting out of the car, and walking slowly to the front door, scared of what could be behind it. I must breathe, and just go in, I said to myself.

As I opened the door, I couldn't hear anything, it was really quiet, but Nick didn't come to the door either.

Something is wrong, I thought. I pushed open the door, but I didn't enter, I waited a moment. "Hello, Nick I am home," I yelled to let it be known I was here. Still no one, that is weird, I thought where are they? As I entered the family room, I saw Nick tied to the chair, and the maids were tied together on the couch, "where are the girls?" I asked trying to keep my voice calm. Nick glanced upward, like he was trying to tell me something. "What?" I said quietly, as I untied them. I heard someone up stairs walking.

"Quick Victoria, leave us, we will be safe here if we are tied, we will pretend to be tied, but you need to get out of here," he demanded.

"I don't think so Nick, thank you, but I am going to put an end to this once and for all," I demanded and stood firm on my words. I left the family room, and went looking.

"Dominic where are you?" I screamed loud enough for anyone in the house to hear. I walked up the stairs slowly; "I know that whoever is up here wants me dead. I know you're up here, why don't you come out and face me," just as I called out, someone hit me in the back of the head, and I went down.

I woke up to Dominic looking down at me, "get away from me, you monster" I screamed as I tried to get up, realizing then that I was tied up. "You monster! Why don't you leave me alone?" I screamed.

"I will once your inheritance is mine, but I can't do that until you are dead, and you leave it to me," he said with a very unhappy glare.

"I will never sign it to you," I screamed. "You have money, why do you need mine?" I asked.

"I am broke, I have lost a lot of my investments over the years, and I have been waiting for you to find yours, but unfortunately you left before you found it," he said.

"I don't have money Dominic, I invested it as soon as I got it, because I knew you would be coming after me," I told him. "Is that why you have been so cruel to me over the years, or is that just how you treat people?" I asked defiantly.

"Actually, Victoria I have always loved you, but I know I can't have you leaving me, if I can't have you no one will," he said. The words hit so hard, I would have swore he hit me with his fist. "Sign this," he ordered.

"No I will never sign, go to hell Dominic" I screamed.

"Get away from her, you monster," Stephan came rushing in, and pushed him away from me.

"Oh, so it is true, you ran away with Stephan, I always knew you had something going on with him, you whore, how could you?" Dominic bellowed. Just as he was spitting his words out, Stephan hit him upside the head, knocking him right to the ground.

"Don't you ever talk to her that way again," he said.

"What the hell," Dominic stood up and asked, "how dare you lay a hand on me," Dominic yelled and lunged at him.

"Stop, please you are going to get hurt," I screamed. I was wiggling my hands, and pulling trying to get them untied, and I finally did. I jumped off the bed and lunged at Dominic, hitting him in the side of the head, "leave him alone!" I screamed. Dominic swung his arm back hitting me and sending me into the French doors, breaking them. I landed on the deck three stories up.

"Victoria are you ok?" Stephan yelled.

"She isn't going to be if she doesn't sign these papers," Dominic yelled and threw the papers and the pen at me.

I stood up, "hey Dominic, look," I said as I ripped up the papers, "Go to hell," I screamed, it felt so good to stand up to him. He lunged at me, with both hands, but I moved over so he wouldn't send me over the balcony. It was him who went over the rail of the three story balcony. “Oh my goodness, I didn’t mean to” I gasped in total shock of what just happened. I didn’t mean for him to go over the edge.

“Victoria, call the cops, now” Stephan demanded.

“Ok,” I said shakily, but I didn’t call the cops, I needed to see what I had done. I looked down over the balcony at Dominic’s lifeless body, I couldn’t help but feel free, and relieved, when I saw he wasn’t moving, he was gone. Was it finally over, was this it? I wondered.

“Victoria, call the cops,” Stephan screamed again.

“Oh, right I am sorry,” I said grabbing the phone. “They are on their way Stephan,” I said as I hung the phone up.

“Stephan are you ok?” I asked as I went up to hug him.

“Yes, are you?” he asked wrapping his arms around me.

“Yes, let’s go down and check on Nick, and the maids,” I said as we walked out of that room.

“Victoria I am so proud of you, you stood up to him, and you ended this,” Stephan said as we walked downstairs.

“Nick,” I called as we entered the family room.

"Yes, we are right here, I am so sorry ma'am, I should've protected you," he said hugging me.

"It's ok, Nick, but where are my girls? I must find them," I said hoping he would know where they were.

"Oh, Miss the girls are fine, they are in a hideaway," he said smiling.

"The hideaway?" I asked confused.

"Oh, I will show you, it is in the side closet, there is a door inside of it that leads to a tunnel inside the house. They are completely fine. I asked one of the other maids to take them there," he said. Relief shot through me. We reached the closet and Nick went inside and got the girls,

"Mommy you're ok," they came running out and said.

"Of course I am babies, I told you I would keep you safe," I said with tears streaming down my cheeks.

"Why are you crying?" Sarah asked.

"They are tears of joy," I said still hugging them.

"Miss Victoria may we speak to you?" a man said from behind us. I turned and it was police officer.

"Yes" I said as I walked over to them. I told them what happened, and so did everyone else.

"Ok, Ma'am, you are very lucky, we have been wanting to catch him ever since he wasn't convicted after he killed his stepmother," the officer said. He wished us luck and left.

"Wow, I can't believe they didn't give us anymore hassle over a man being dead," I said.

"Victoria, thank goodness you are alright, we tried to get here as fast as we could," Natasha came running in and said, while hugging me.

"It's ok, how are you guys?" I asked.

"We are great, we had an awesome time, until we got a call from Nick saying Luke had taken you, so we left as soon as possible, but I think we are a little late, we missed all the excitement," she said.

"Yes you did, but it's over" I said. "Dominic is gone, now the only way he can hurt us, is if he haunts us from the afterlife," I said with a laugh.

"Ok, I think this calls for ice cream," Nick said.

"Yes, perfect idea," we all agreed.

After we had ice cream, I tucked the girls into bed, and went to see how Nicole was doing. "Nicole, how was your day?" I asked as I went in her room.

"I am alright, how is Stephanie's arm?" she asked.

"Her arm is fine, they are both good, I think they are happier knowing that he is gone," I said as I sat next to her on her bed.

"Victoria, I am so sorry I wasn't here to care for the girls and you," she said as the tears began to stream down her cheeks.

"Nicole stop crying and look at me, I am very happy you went with Natasha. And I am even more happy you weren't here today. Because I know you would've gotten yourself killed trying to protect me," I said hugging her.

"Yeah, you are right about that, I will not let anyone hurt you again," she said.

"I know baby, but you are still a child and you need to be able to be carefree, and happy, so let's not worry about this anymore. Let's think about our futures. You will start school this coming fall, and so will the girls. You will get chances to go on dates, and make friends, and that my dear is all you need to think about," I told her with a smile, hoping she would believe me.

"Ok, Victoria, thank you," she said.

"Good night, if you need me come get me," I told her as I left her room.

I am so happy this is all over, I thought to myself. I sat there on the edge of my bed, wondering, thinking, hoping, and praying this was it. But I have a strong feeling, something worse is headed our way. I wanted so bad to dream of the future and make plans, but I think my mother's and grandfather's past is going to come to the near present.

"Victoria, there you are." Stephan said as he came in and kissed me. The moment his lips touched mine, I couldn't help but feel like everything was better.

"Stephan, hi how are you doing?" I asked.

"I am wonderful Victoria. Dominic is gone, you and the girls are safe, that's all I have ever wanted. Well maybe one more thing, but in time," he said with a smile.

"Oh yeah, what is that one thing," I asked hoping he would say it was me.

"It's you Victoria, but I will not pressure you into anything, when the time is right," he said holding my hand.

"Stephan, I love you, I always have, I have always loved you. I was always so scared to admit it, until tonight when I thought I had lost you, and I will not go another day, without telling you that I do love you. I am so sorry I never told you," I said with tears streaming down my cheeks.

"Victoria I love you too, and I always have," he said.

I leaned back onto the bed, he leaned down on me, kissing me so passionately, so lovely. I couldn't help, but opening my heart and soul to him, he is the only man I have ever truly loved and wanted.

"Victoria are you sure?" he asked as he slid his hand under me to take my panties down.

"Yes, I am sure," I said with so much ecstasy, I couldn't help it. I wanted him so bad. As we made love I truly felt the magic, the love Stephan was sending me, was undeniable. Afterwards we lay there in each other's arms. How long we had waited to be together, it seemed like eternity, and now we could be together.

"Stephan are you alright?" I asked to break the silence.

"Yes, Victoria I am the happiest man on earth," he said. The stress from the day had drained us both, we had fallen asleep and I didn't realize it until I woke up.

"Victoria, good morning," Natasha said as she came in, "oh my, I'm sorry I didn't mean to interrupt" she said as she quickly turned around and left the room. Both Stephan and I laughed, we couldn't help it.

"I am going to dress" he said with a laugh. I grabbed a shirt and pants, and as I was putting my clothes on Natasha came back in.

"Hey I am so sorry, I didn't think he was in here," she said.

"It's ok, we fell asleep last night, and I just woke up when you came in," I said laughing. "I feel like a teenager getting busted by my mom," I said laughing.

"So how are you this morning?" she asked.

"I am wonderful, our nightmare is over," I said. "Let's go get breakfast," I said as I led the way out of our room.

Down at breakfast, everyone seemed to be very happy. Sarah was telling knock, knock jokes to Nicole and Stephanie, and then they would laugh hysterically, it made me laugh as well. Natasha was making business plans on her laptop, and Stephan was talking on his phone, making business plans as well. So is this what it is like to live in a normal family? I wondered to myself.

"Miss Victoria, would you like a cup of coffee?" Nick asked holding a cup of coffee up to me.

"Oh yes, I would Nick, thank you so much," I said accepting the coffee. As I sat there drinking my coffee, I couldn't believe everything was over, my nightmare had finally ended. "Sarah and Stephanie, how would you like to go to the animal shelter, and get a dog?" I asked them.

"Oh yes, can we please?" they begged.

"Yes, after breakfast we will go," I said. I loved seeing the joy in their eyes.

"Mom, we are done. Can we go upstairs and get dressed?" the girls asked.

"Yes, but I am going to finish my coffee, and eat a little breakfast, then we can go, is that alright girls?" I asked.

"Ok, thank you" they said as they ran up the stairs to get dressed.

"Victoria are you sure want to get a dog?" Natasha asked.

"Yeah, I think it will be good for them, they have been asking for a dog for a long time," I said.

"Ok, well is it alright if we all go?" Natasha asked.

"Actually, Natasha I would like to spend the day with just the girls, they have been through so much, I think this would be good for them," I said, hoping I wouldn't hurt her feelings.

"I think that is a wonderful idea Victoria, don't you Natasha?" Stephan asked more as an order to her than a question.

"Yeah, it is," she said with a soft smile, trying to hide her real feelings.

"Thank you both for understanding," I said as I got up to go get ready.

As I was getting dressed, the girls came running in and asked if I was ready yet. "Almost girls," I said. "Sarah where is Nicole?" I asked.

"She is getting dressed, but she is really excited too," Sarah said.

"Good, I am thinking we should get a big but friendly dog," I told them.

"Yeah, I love big dogs," Stephanie said.

"Good, are you two ready?" I asked.

"Yes, let's go" Sarah said impatiently.

"Ok you go down stairs, and I will get Nicole," I told them. As they left the room, I heard their giggles, and excitement, it made me so happy.

"Nicole are you ready honey?' I asked as I entered her room.

"Yes, I was just writing in my journal," she said as she put it away.

"Honey we can wait if you want to finish," I said.

"Oh, that's ok, I am done," she said. "Let's go" she said full of excitement.

"Ok, let's go get a dog," I said as we left the room, and headed down stairs.

"Victoria are you ok?" Nicole asked half way down the stairs.

"Yes, honey I am great I have three wonderful daughters, and a great new home, with endless possibilities, so yes honey I am wonderful," I said.

"Good, because I am very happy here too" she said. The girls were waiting for us by the door, when we got down there.

"Bye," I yelled as we left to go get a dog.

"Mom, what are we going to name our new dog?" Stephanie asked.

"I'm not sure what would you guys like to name it?" I asked hoping it would distract them long enough to get to the shelter.

"How about Snickers?" Nicole asked.

"I like that" I said.

"We do too, it's our favorite candy bar," the girls said.

"That's mine too" Nicole said.

"Well girls, we are here," I said. They all yelled with excitement. "Ok, easy girls, remember we need to use our indoor voices" I said, laughing.

"Ok, we are sorry," Sarah said.

As we walked inside, we saw many dogs, and of course the girls wanted to take them all home. "Mom, how can we pick just one, they all need homes?" Stephanie said.

"I know baby, but we need to let other families have one too," I said.

"Ok," she said as she ran to catch up to her sisters.

"Victoria, what about this one? It's a girl, and she's very young, and she has the softest brown eyes I have ever seen," Nicole said standing in front of a chocolate lab puppy.

"Oh, I like her; she is perfect" I said, opening the cage door. The puppy came running out and jumped up on

Nicole's legs. When she knelt down to pet the puppy, I saw a sparkle in her eye that I had never seen before and I knew then that I had to get that puppy. "Sarah, Stephanie what do you think of this one?" I asked them as they came up.

"We like her, but we like this one too, Mom," they said moving to the side to show me, this very cute little black furry dog.

"Girls she is very cute too," I couldn't say no. "Ok, girls I have an idea, but I will need all of your help," I said before I told them my idea, "so will you help?" I asked.

"Of course we will help, what is your idea?" they asked knowing what I would say.

"Let's take them both home," I told them. They jumped up and down with excitement.

"Thank you, thank you, thank you" they chanted still jumping.

"Ok, girls, well let's calm down for a minute," I said to them trying to make them calm down so we could ask the man how much. "Let's go and find someone to help us, so we can take the dogs home," I said.

We finally found a man sitting behind a desk, in a chair, almost asleep. "Excuse me, Sir," I said very loudly.

"Oh, yes what can I do for you ma'am?" he asked.

"I am sorry to disturb you but, I would like to take these two dogs home," I said showing him the dogs.

"Oh right, yeah I can do that," he said shuffling through some papers, like he was looking for something. "Please give me a moment while I find the application," he said.

"Excuse me sir, I don't mean to question your business or you, but what do you mean application? I just moved here, and my girls and I have been through hell, and I wanted to do something special for them," I asked.

"Well ma'am, I am sorry but here, we have people fill out an application for a dog, and after we screen you we figure out if the animal will be a match for you and your lifestyle," he said.

"Oh, sir I am sorry but I just moved here, and if you would like I will show you our house. It is all fenced, my grandfather Joseph Strong had the place built, and it is top of the line everything. I promise you these dogs will have the best home possible, please sir I am begging you please don't break my girl's hearts," I begged.

"Ma'am you said your grandfather is Joseph Strong?" he asked.

"Yes, sir," I said a little confused.

"So you are Mary Ann's daughter," he asked skeptically?

"Yes, I am, what does that have to do with this?" I asked maybe a little too harsh.

"Oh, I'm sorry Ma'am, but I was a good friend to your mother, so please take the dogs. Any daughter of hers, I am sure will give proper care to any animal," he said smiling.

"Thank you, may I ask your name?" I asked.

"Oh, I am sorry ma'am, my name is John Sully," he said holding out his hand for me to shake.

"It is nice to meet you John Sully, I am Victoria Strong, and these are my girls Sarah, Stephanie and Nicole" I said pointing to each of them.

"Well it is an honor to meet you," he said. "You may have the dogs, I won't charge you for them," he said.

"No I insist, we will pay for the dogs," I said handing him $200.00.

"Thank you, but you don't need to" he said.

"I know but I want to," I said still holding the money.

"Ok, well thank you," he said.

"Well girls, what do you say we take these two puppies home," I said.

"Ok, let's go home" they said with permanent smiles on their faces. As we walked outside with the dogs, I asked the girls what we were going to name them again.

"I want to name her Snickers," Nicole said pointing to the chocolate lab.

"Ok, Nicole we can call her Snickers. Sarah and Stephanie what do you want to name her?" I asked pointing to the little black puppy.

"Can we call her Blacky?" they asked.

"Ok, we will call her Blacky," I said. The girls all seemed very happy on the way home.

As we pulled in the driveway, I saw Stephan and Natasha standing outside, they seemed to be arguing about something. I parked the car and went up to see what they were talking about, but as soon as they saw me, they exchanged a look, and pretended to be completely happy again. "Hey, what is going on, I saw you guys arguing when I pulled up," I asked hoping one of them would tell me.

"Oh, we were just discussing the party we are going to throw," Natasha burst out and said.

"Yeah, that's what we were talking about, we couldn't agree on a time and date," Stephan said trying to make me believe him.

"Ok, well guys we've got two puppies," I said as I stepped back so the girls could show them. "This little brown eyed beauty is Snickers," I said pointing to her, "and this little girl is Blacky, we couldn't say no to either of them," I said with a giggle.

"Well, we were betting you would come back with the whole damn place," Stephan said. We laughed. He was right, I did have a soft spot for animals.

"Girls let's go inside, and let the puppies explore their new home," I said and began to make my way into the house.

The girls immediately ran upstairs to make a bed in their room for Blacky. "Nicole, where do you want Snickers to sleep?" I asked her.

"Victoria if you don't mind, I would like you to make Snickers your dog," she said.

"What honey, I thought you fell in love at first sight with her?" I asked her.

"Yes I did, because I remember something I was told about labs, they are very loyal dogs, and are very protective. She will be a great toy for the girls and I, but she will be your companion," Nicole stated.

"Nicole that is very sweet of you, but how about we share her, she can stay in my room if you want and you can teach tricks, and play with her," I said hoping she would like that idea.

"Ok, I like that idea," she said as she went upstairs to play with the puppies.

"Nick?" I called as I went into the kitchen.

"Yes, Victoria what is it, is something wrong?" he asked as he walked up to me.

"Nothing is wrong, but I am very concerned, have you heard or seen anything odd from Natasha and Stephan?" I asked him hoping he could answer the question.

"No ma'am I haven't, they have been in the study most of the day," he said.

"Ok, thank you Nick, and could you please keep this to yourself," I asked.

"Of course," he said and smiled and went back to doing his thing. There is something definitely going on between them, and I don't know what it is, I thought to myself.

"Victoria, there you are" Stephan said as he walked up and kissed me. There was something different in the way he kissed me, it wasn't personal.

"Stephan is there something going on that I don't know about?" I asked him.

"No honey, you are just being paranoid, you have been through so much, you need to relax," he said rubbing my shoulders.

"Maybe you are right," I said. "What are the girls doing?" I asked him.

"They are upstairs playing with the puppies," he said still rubbing my shoulders.

"Ok, well I am going to go up and see them, and make sure they get ready for dinner. I was thinking we could order a pizza and relax tonight," I said hoping he would like that idea.

"That sounds wonderful," he said. "You go check on the girls and I will order a pizza, I think Natasha is going back home tonight. She said something about having to finalize the new business plan," he said.

"Oh, I didn't know, I hope everything is ok," I said.

"Oh I am sure it is," he said trying to reassure me.

"Ok, well I will be back down in a minute," I said.

"No, please Victoria I will bring up the pizza and stuff, you just relax," he said as he kissed me, before I left to see the girls.

"Thank you Stephan," I said. He really was wonderful to me, always thinking of me.

"Girls, how are the puppies getting along so far?" I asked as I came into their room.

"They are good, they love playing tug of war," Sarah said.

"Well girls how does pizza and a movie sound for dinner?" I asked.

"Yeah, we love pizza, can we watch the Little Mermaid, please, please?" Stephanie begged.

"We'll see honey, but first we need to clean up this room, so we can eat in here," I said as I started picking up toys.

"Ok, but can Blacky and Snickers have pizza too, please?" Stephanie asked.

"No, sweetie I am sorry, but dogs shouldn't eat people food, it's bad for them," I said.

"Ok, I don't want them to get sick," she said.

"Girls, pizza is here," Stephan sang as he came in the room. "We got pepperoni pizza, with lots of cheesy breadsticks," he said.

"Yum, I am starving," Nicole said.

"Oh, yeah and there is Coca-cola for our drink," he said.

"Thank you Stephan." I said as I began to put pizza on the girl's plates. "Oh Stephan, we are watching the Little

Mermaid, I hope you don't mind," I said with a laugh knowing he would be thrilled to watch it.

"Sounds good to me, I will put it in the DVD player," he said as he got up to start the movie. As we sat there and ate pizza, and watched the movie, the girls were very quiet. Blacky laid right next to them, and Snickers laid with her head on my lap, it was very nice to feel like a normal family again.

"Victoria, I think the girls are sleeping," Stephan said in a very quiet voice.

"You're right they are, let's put them in their beds, and go to our room," he said. Our room, the sound of that was nice, I would have never guessed that Stephan and I would be together, I had loved him since we were kids and now we could finally be together.

"Ok, that's sounds good," I said as I picked up Sarah to put her in her bed, and he grabbed Stephanie to do the same. "I will wake Nicole" I said, looking at her lying on the sofa.

"No, let her sleep, she will be fine there, she always sleeps better near the girls," he said. He was right about that, Nicole was very protective of those little girls. She would do anything for them, and me, I thought to myself.

Once we lay in bed, I realized how tired I was. “Victoria, I love you,” Stephan said.

“I love you too, Stephan,” I said kissing him good night. As I laid there in his arms, I wondered if it would always be this way, happy, safe and wonderful. How weird for the longest time, I had wondered if it would always be that way, living in a dark, cold home, where I was always scared, and walking on egg shells, and now I was wondering if it would always be like this happy and wonderful. I fell asleep in Stephan’s arms, dreaming of the future, but I woke up to a shocking realization.

I woke up, and Stephan wasn’t in bed, I got up and put my robe on. He is probably making coffee, I thought. As I walked out of my room, I heard him talking in his bedroom, he was on the phone. I was about to open the door, when I heard him say, “Don’t worry Victoria has no clue, and soon it will all be ours. I love you so please don’t worry, Victoria thinks I am all about her, and she is so happy right now she won’t see it coming.” Oh my goodness, who was he talking to, how could I have been so stupid? I thought to myself. What would all be his, who was he working with? I wondered, I have to find out, but I can’t let him know, I know. Then I heard a woman’s voice, he wasn't on the phone, there was a woman in there, I waited for her to talk again.

I heard her say, "I love you too Stephan, but we need to get this done soon, I hate pretending to be her sister, and best friend." It was Natasha, but how could she be pretending, I wondered. I listened some more, and she said "I thought once we got Dominic out of the picture this would be easy, but now it's getting more complicated, and Nicole now remembers. But I think I have her under control, it's really quite pathetic, poor Nicole will keep our secret to protect them, I threatened to kill the girls and Victoria, if she told".

I have to leave, I must get the girls and Nicole out of here, I thought, but how, I don't want to run anymore. I need answers, I must figure out how they have been playing me. Just when you think the nightmare is over, a new one begins, I thought to myself, but this time I will stand up and fight them, I will not be their puppet anymore.

I walked in the kitchen and was surprised to see Luke, "I thought you were dead," I said sternly as I grabbed the bat from behind the door.

"Look, I am not here to hurt you, I never wanted to. That night I tried to kidnap you, I was trying to protect you from Stephan and Natasha. I have been working undercover to find my children. I am very sorry for what I have done, but I found the answers I have been looking for, and you need to see these," he said holding out a big envelope. I took the envelope, and looked inside, there were pictures.

As I looked at those pictures from Luke, I was shocked. There were pictures of the girls and Violet, when Sarah was a baby. "How do you have these?" I asked as I held up the first picture.

"Please, Victoria look at the rest," Luke told me, in a very soft voice. I looked at the next picture; it was Natasha and Stephan in each other's arms. They were wrapped in a sheet, at Natasha's old house.

"What are you trying to do to me Luke?" I asked with anger dripping off my words.

"Look Victoria, you have no reason to trust me, but I have been working for Dominic, but it's not for the reasons you may think. I started working for Dominic when you left with the girls," he said.

"Why would it matter to you if I left with the girls?" I asked not sure of what he might say.

"Victoria, I am the girl's father," he said. The words hit me like a baseball bat.

"What? How, I mean, I heard you died, after you left them because you were too heartbroken to care for them?" I said surprised.

"Yes, I did fake my death, but not for the reasons you think. I did it, so Dominic would quit trying to have me killed, I went to him about a year after Violet's death, because I wanted the girls back, and that's when I found out about their inheritance from Dominic. He said that was the only reason I was back, but I never knew about it, until he told me," he said.

"What? I never knew about that?" I said full of confusion.

"Victoria, you need to believe me, you and the girls are in grave danger. Stephan and Natasha have been scamming you. They want your money, and everything. I couldn't believe what he was saying, but after what I had just heard from Stephan and Natasha, I had no choice but to believe him.

"Ok, I do believe you, but I don't know what to do, should I leave or should I play the game they are playing?" I asked.

"Play the game, but beat them," he said. "Oh yeah, just so you know, I am not going to take the girls, or the inheritance. I am only here to protect you and them. I want to be a part of their lives' but their safety is more important, so please don't think I am scamming you," he said.

I heard footsteps coming down the stairs," Luke you must leave, I can't have them find you, if they do then you will be in even more danger," I said hoping he would go out through the kitchen.

"Ok Victoria, but I want to finish this conversation, can you meet later tonight?" he asked.

"Yes, I will, let's meet at the gas station," I told him.

"Ok, 9:00 pm," he said.

"Ok, thank you Luke," I said as he left.

"Victoria, are you in here?" Natasha called from the living room.

"Yes, I am in the kitchen," I called back to her.

"Oh good, there is someone I want you to meet," Natasha said as she came into the kitchen.

"Ok, who is it?" I asked trying to be natural.

"This is Kelly," she said moving to the side, to reveal the woman to me. I couldn't believe it, it was the woman from the gas station. What is Natasha trying to pull? I wondered.

"Well hello, Kelly" I said as I extended my hand to greet her. There was no way I was going to let Natasha and

Stephan get away with this, so I am going to play along, I thought. "Natasha, not to be rude but is there a reason why I am meeting Kelly," I asked softly, trying to be sweet.

"Oh, how silly of me," she said with a laugh. "Kelly is going to be my assistant, so I don't have to do everything all the time, she is going to be here living with us," Natasha continued. What? Did she think I was stupid? I wasn't going to sit back and let them run my house.

"That is wonderful Natasha I am so happy for you," I said with the best fake sincere smile I could find inside myself.

"Victoria, did Natasha tell you her great news?" Stephan asked as he came in the kitchen.

"Yes, she did," I said still trying not to blow my own cover. "Natasha have I met her before? she looks familiar," I asked trying to feel them out.

"Oh, maybe she has done work for me before," she said.

"Ok, well it's wonderful to meet you Kelly, but I hope you don't mind I must be getting the girls," I said as I left. As I walked up the stairs to get the girls, I couldn't help but wonder if Luke was for real, after all, he is the man who broke my ribs, and tried to kill me the other night.

Relax Victoria, everything will be alright, I heard a voice say. I turned to see who was there but no one was. That is puzzling, I thought. I must be just very stressed, and concerned, or my soul is speaking to me, telling me what to do, I couldn't help but giggle to myself. I seriously was losing my mind, not only was I talking to myself, I was laughing at myself now. I said to myself. I wish Violet and mother were here; maybe they could help me, or tell me what to do. I was half way up the stairs, I heard Snickers coming up behind me, and she was limping. As I bent down to pick her up, I felt something hit me in the back of the head; I fell down, and rolled down the stairs.

"Mom, Victoria are you alright?" Sarah and Nicole yelled as they came down the stairs. "Aunt Natasha, hurry, quick come here, its Mom" Sarah yelled. Natasha came running, Stephan was right behind her.

"What happened?" Natasha cried as she bent down to feel for a pulse on my body.

"We don't know. We heard a crash, and then we saw Victoria at the bottom of the stairs, and Snickers was sitting next to her."

I was standing there watching them, my body lay there motionless on the floor, but my spirit, or ghost was present. I kept yelling at them, telling them I was ok, I just fell but they couldn't hear me. I tried to touch Sarah, but my hand went right through her, I was a ghost, but how, I couldn't die yet, what about my girls, and Nicole, who was going to look after them? I had to find a way to get back to them, I screamed to myself.

"Nicole, take the girls upstairs," Stephan ordered.

"Yes, of course" Nicole said as she started up the stairs with the girls.

"Nicole, what is happening?" Stephanie cried.

"It's ok honey, Victoria just fell and now she needs a doctor, but it's going to be ok, I promise," Nicole said as she picked her up and carried her up the stairs.

"Call the doctor now," Stephan yelled to Natasha.

"Ok," she said as she picked up the phone to dial the number. "Wait Stephan, maybe if we wait, it will be too late, and then we are in the clear, we never have to worry again," Natasha said. How could she be so cruel, we were sisters, she has been my best friend forever, how could she now be this completely different person? I wondered.

"Look, Nikki I told you, I would go along with this, just so I could protect Natasha, but I will not let you, kill Victoria, I may have been deceiving her, but I still love her," Stephan screamed at her. Why was he calling her Nikki? and referring to Natasha as if she wasn't there.

"What the hell was going on," I screamed, hoping they could hear me.

"Fine, Stephan but I swear if you screw this up for me, I will kill your precious Natasha. Do you think Victoria is going to love you once she finds out, that you and Natasha have been scamming her out of her money? And that Natasha really isn't her sister, it was a scam you created, so Natasha could keep Violets inheritance?" she screamed at him. What was she talking about, Natasha wasn't rich or my sister, it was a scam they created to keep the money? This was all too confusing.

"Damn it, Nikki call the doctor," Stephan demanded.

"Ok, relax I am," she said as she dialed the number, and told the doctor there was an accident and to come quick. It was amazing she actually sounded sincere on the phone, she actually sounded like she cared. Who was this Nikki woman who looked just like Natasha, I wondered? "The doctor should be here in a minute," she told Stephan.

"Good, now please get away from her, I don't trust you, and I don't want you to do anything to hurt her," he said in a tone more than threatening.

"Oh, don't worry I won't do anything to her, I promise" she said as she held up her right hand, as if she was in court or something. Maybe this ghost stuff, was exactly what I needed to find out the answers I needed, I thought.

"Lord Stephan, do you know what happened?" the doctor asked as he began to examine my body, lying there on the floor.

"No, I don't. We heard the girls scream and we came running and found her here, we were going to move her to the couch, but I was afraid to risk it," Stephan said to the doctor. He sounded so sincere; every word out of his mouth was dripping with sorrow. Maybe he does care, I thought.

"Well let's move her to a bed," the doctor said. "We must be very careful, support the head, neck and back," he warned.

"Yes, doctor. Nick?" Stephan called.

"Yes, Stephan what can I do for you?" Nick asked.

"I need your help moving Victoria to a bed," Stephan asked.

"Of course," Nick said as he came over to help move me. As they moved me to the bed, the doctor began examining my body, and all he could figure out is I was in a coma. My vitals were good, and everything looked good, the doctor told Stephan.

"I will send a nurse over to monitor her twenty-four seven, until she wakes, but right now it's up to her," the doctor said.

"Thank you doctor," Stephan said as he shook his hand.

"Oh isn't this wonderful, now we will have another person in this house snooping around, and getting in the way of our plans," Nikki said.

"Get over it Nikki, Victoria needs the care, and damn it, she will get it," he screamed at her. "Just leave me alone," he yelled.

"Fine, I am going out, but don't do anything stupid, or grow some compassion. We have a deal, and I will kill Natasha if you break that deal," she warned as she left.

"Oh Victoria, I am so sorry, I never meant for any of this to happen, it all started out as just a scam, no one was supposed to get hurt. It has all gotten out of hand, I am so sorry," Stephan cried as he sat there next to me holding my hand.

"Victoria?" I heard a woman's voice say. I turned to see, and it was my mother. "What, how, I mean oh my goodness, how is this possible" I cried hugging her.

"Victoria, we don't have much time, you need to listen to me," she said.

"Ok, but I don't understand," I began to say.

"It's ok, I am the one that hit you so you would fall, I am sorry, but that was the only way I could connect with you, I promise you will be fine," she said.

"Ok, what is it?" I asked still very confused.

"When you wake up, you must pretend you know nothing, and you must trust Luke, he is the girl's father. He will be the only one you can trust right now," she said.

"Ok, but how do you know about him?" I asked.

"His father is Nick your butler, and he was sent to keep an eye on you and Violet, after I passed, but he messed up and fell in love with her. That is not important, you need to focus," she said.

"Ok, what do you need me to do?" I asked.

"Follow me," she said as she started to go upstairs.

"Ok, where are we going?" I asked.

"To my bedroom, there is another diary in there, and that will tell you everything, but you can't let them know about it. I am going to show you where it is, then when you wake up, you are going to get it, and take it to Luke, please" she said.

"Ok, I will but when will I wake up?" I asked.

"That is up to you, but I advise you to be quick about it, the longer you are out, the harder it will be to wake," she warned. "Here it is," she said as she lifted the loose floor board, and there was the diary. "I hid it here so no one would find it," she said. "I am sorry but you are on your own now, I can't help you any more, this part is up to you," she said.

"Mom, please wait, I miss you, and I don't want you to leave," I begged.

"I know baby, I love you too, but I have to go, there are rules to me guiding you, and if I do too much I could change the course of time, and I can't risk it," she said as she hugged me and kissed my cheek.

Now what was I supposed to do, what is so important in the diary, that she had to put me in a coma to find? I wondered. "Victoria, please wake up, the girls need you, I need you," I heard a voice say. It was Nicole she was crying. Why was she so sad, what was wrong with her, I asked myself. "Victoria, there is something I need to tell you, but I don't know how, I am so sorry Victoria," she cried, as she held my hand. I wanted so bad to run to her, but I still didn't know how. "Victoria, you need to wake up, I need you, I don't know what to do, I am pregnant, and I am so scared, and Natasha and Stephan are plotting against you," she cried. Pregnant, how could she be pregnant? I screamed. I need to get back to my girls now, I screamed louder than I have ever done, hoping the spirits would hear me and send me back to them, and moments later I realized I was awake.

"Nicole?" I whispered, "Shh, let's not let them know I woke up, I can hear you, and I promise I will make everything alright I promise," I whispered to her. She was in shock," I am sorry I scared you all, but I tripped and hit my head, then I fell down the stairs, but I am ok. I know about Natasha and Stephan, but please don't say anymore right now I can't risk them knowing I know," I told her.

"Ok," she said with tears streaming down her face.

"Ok, I am going to pretend to be asleep some more, but I am going to act like I am starting to wake up, and when I squeeze your hand, yell for the nurse to come in," I advised her.

"Ok, Victoria I am so sorry," she cried.

"It's ok baby, I will take care of everything" I said to her as I closed my eyes.

I squeezed her hand just as I told her I would, and she called for the nurse. The nurse came in, did some of my vitals, and then I opened my eyes slowly. I was actually very groggy feeling. "Victoria, do you know where you are at?" the nurse asked.

"Yes, I am at home in riverside at the Strong Mansion," I said.

"Yes, you are right, how many fingers am I holding up?" the nurse asked as she held up 3 fingers.

"Three, can I have something to drink, my throat is very dry?" I said in a raspy voice.

"Of course, here is some water but sips please, don't drink too much at once," the nurse warned.

"Victoria my love, are you alright?" Stephan came rushing in and asked me.

"Yes, I am, I am just a little tired is all," I said.

"Oh, Victoria we were so worried, how did you fall?" he asked as he sat there holding my hand.

"I just tripped is all, I bent down to pick up Snickers, and lost my balance," I said with a little giggle.

"Well I am glad you are alright, you should rest," he said leaning down to kiss my forehead.

"I will," I said as he got up to leave. "Stephan is there any way I could talk to Natasha?" I asked hoping I could figure out what had happened.

"I think Natasha left for a bit, she was pacing back and forth, so I told her to go for a walk," he said. I knew he was lying, he has done this odd thing with his lip when he was lying, although I haven't seen him do that since we were children, and I caught him stealing apples from the church apple tree.

"Ok, well when she returns will you tell her to come see me? I want to make sure she is alright; I know this has probably scared her half to death," I said trying to hide anything in my voice that would say otherwise.

"Oh of course, my love" Stephan said with the saddest look in his eyes, this must really be bothering him, I wondered. No, I can't think about him right now; I said to myself, I have other things to take care of.

I must have nodded off, because I woke up to Stephan yelling at Natasha or Nikki or whoever that woman is. I couldn't quite make out what he was upset about, but he sounded furious with her. What could he be so upset about? Oh no did she hurt Natasha? I thought. It's weird, I know Natasha and Stephan have been betraying me, but I still cared about them, I still care if they are hurt, or worse, I don't want to think about the worse things now. I know what I need to do, I need to see if what I dreamt was real or a dream, but how could I get to Mother's bedroom without them knowing. I could ask Nicole, I thought but she has her own problems to worry about, and she is pregnant. I still can't figure out how she could be pregnant, she was only almost 16, she is too young.

I looked around hoping she was still nearby and sure enough she was, she was sitting in the chair across the room fast asleep. “Nicole?” I said in a loud whisper hoping it was just loud enough for her to hear and no one else. She moved a bit, but didn’t wake up.” Nicole” I said in a little bit louder whisper.

“Oh, what?” she said in a very groggy, half asleep type tone.

“Nicole, I need you to please wake up, I must talk to you, please” I begged hoping she would wake up.

“Yes, Lady Victoria, I am sorry I tried to stay awake, but I must have fallen asleep,” she said.

“It’s ok, I need to know are you ok baby? and how on earth are you pregnant? I’m not mad, I am just very confused, I don’t understand how you are with child,” I said trying to keep my composure, and not scare her.

“Ma’am I am very sorry, I didn’t mean to, I tried to stop him,” she said as she started to cry.

“Hey honey it’s ok, please don’t cry, I just want to know,” I said as I rubbed her hand. “Who is the father?” I asked hoping I wouldn’t upset her any more than she already was.

“Victoria please don’t be mad, but it is Dominic,” she said as the tears streamed down her cheeks.

"Oh, baby it's alright, I promise, it will be ok," I said still holding her. "Nicole, I don't want to upset you, but I need to know, did he force it upon you?" I asked not sure what answer I wanted to hear.

"Yes, Miss Victoria, I am so sorry, I tried to stop him, but he was drunk, and he is a lot stronger than me," she cried.

"It's alright, I understand, but I need to know how far along you are, almost afraid of that answer. I am about six months," she said.

"What? Six months, oh my goodness, honey we need to get you some proper prenatal care," I said still in shock.

"I have been taking vitamins, and when we were at Dominic's house, I received care," she said.

"Ok, honey well we will handle this anyway you want," I said.

"OK, thank you Miss. Victoria, thank you so much," she said as the tears started to diminish.

"Nicole, I need you to do me a favor, without anyone knowing, can you do it for me?" I asked.

"Yes, whatever you need," she said.

"I need you to sneak up to my mother's old bedroom, and there is a loose floor board, and under that is a diary, please bring it to me," I asked.

"Yes, of course I will do it right now," she said.

"Ok, but please be careful, please!" I begged.

"I will, I promise" she said as she got up to leave.

I couldn't help but be scared for her, what is she going to do with a baby? I wondered. I will figure this out, I have to, I need to for her. I couldn't help but blame myself for her predicament. He was my husband, and I was supposed to protect her, I screamed inside myself, where only I could hear the pain. I wish Mother was here again, maybe she could help me and tell me what to do, no stop with this self pity party, I screamed at myself.

I heard a light knock on the door. "Who is it, I called?"

"Ma'am, it is me Nick," the voice said.

"Oh, please come in Nick," I said.

"Miss Victoria I must tell you something," he said as he came in. He seemed very upset.

"Nick, what is wrong?" I asked in a quiet voice.

"Ma'am, that woman out there is not Natasha, she looks just like her, but it is not her," he said.

"Nick, I know I heard everything when I was knocked out, it was the strangest thing, I could hear everyone, but my body wouldn't let me wake up," I said.

"Miss Victoria what do you need me to do?" he asked?

"I need you to pretend you know nothing, and just go along with things," I said in a very serious tone, "now please go and act normal," I said hoping he could do it.

I must have dozed off again, because I woke up to Snickers crawling up on the bed. "Oh, hey Snickers, what are you doing girl?" I asked knowing she wasn't going to answer. There was something about this dog, that was almost magical, but I couldn't figure it out.

"Victoria," Nicole said as she came rushing in, "I found it," she said in a much quieter voice.

"Oh, good honey, thank you, but honey now I need you to go upstairs and keep an eye on the girls," I said.

"Oh you are awake Victoria, I was wondering how you were doing," Nikki came in and said.

"Yes, how are you? Stephan told me, you were distraught with worry so he told you to go for a walk, I am so sorry, I worried" I said in a very sweet voice.

"I'm just glad you are alright," she said bending down to hug me.

"Yes, I am all right, thank you for always caring about me," I said.

"You know I can't help but worry, and care about you, we are sisters after all," she said.

"Yes we are, I am still shocked about that, things have happened so fast, it's hard to keep up with it all," I said trying to cover up any uncertainties in my voice.

"Victoria, you should get some rest," she said hoping to sound sincere. I couldn't believe it was almost morning; I was in a comatose state for most of the day, and I feel even more confused than, I did before, I thought to myself.

I tossed and turned most of the night, and awoke to Nick putting a letter under my pillow. "Nick, what are you doing?" I asked with confusion.

"Sorry, ma'am but there was a quest here earlier and he asked me slip this to you," Nick said pulling the letter out from under the pillow.

"Nick, who is it from?" I asked as fear came over me. It was like I was fearing Dominic again, but this time it was an even worse fear, the fear of not knowing who to fear or even to fear.

"Easy Miss Victoria, it's from Luke, he came by yesterday, but was unable to see you," Nick said.

"Oh, I completely forgot, I was supposed to meet him yesterday," I said.

"Miss Victoria, I think you should read the letter. He sounded very intent that it was urgent," Nick said.

"Yes, of course Nick, but could I get some privacy for it please," I asked hoping not to sound untrusting.

"Oh of course ma'am, please excuse me," he said and left. I opened the letter and began to read it.

Dear Victoria.

I stopped at the mansion after you didn't show up for our meeting, I was worried. Once I got there Nick told me of the accident, but I can't help but wonder if an accident was indeed what happened. I must tell you something, before you hear it from someone else and think I too am deceiving you. I am Nick, your butler's son, that is how I came to know Violet, I was sent to watch over you two, but I became involved with Violet, and fell in love with her. Do not confuse this with any type of regret, I do not regret anything I ever did with Violet, I loved her beyond belief, and I am happy that I got to experience that with her. Unfortunately she did die, but that is in the past, and I have gotten over it. Anyway, I wanted you to know about my father, I am sorry if you think I lied but that was not the intention, I didn't want to risk Stephan or Natasha finding out. There is a woman who looks identical to Natasha but she is not Natasha, she is Nikki, and she is very dangerous, you must be very cautious around her.

I just became aware of the scam that Natasha and Stephan pulled. It happened right after Violet's death. A letter went to Natasha by mistake, but it was clearly stated that Violet and you were inheriting lots of money and a very large estate, but Natasha became jealous, and decided to change the documents into her name, and her and Stephan realized that their plan wouldn't work. Because Nick and all the staff here knew there were two children possibly three, and once Natasha found that out, she knew she had to change the plan somehow., She really does care about you and so does Stephan, but do not confuse care with loyalty or love, they are planning on taking the estate and money. They have both made very poor investment choices, kind of like Dominic did, and this Nikki girl will try and kill you to get her share. Lucky for you, she found out about their plan, and found out she and Natasha are actually identical twins. All she wants is money, and revenge on Natasha for never coming to find her once she learned of her, which was about a year after she left the orphanage. A letter from their mother came and told her of everything. I am sorry I have to tell you all of this in a letter, but I needed you to know as soon as possible. I really think you should get away for a weekend so we can meet and discuss everything, and you and the girls will be safe.

Please have Nick contact me, with anything you need, or when you want to meet.

Wow, that is a lot of information to take in all at once, but luckily I already knew most of it. I cannot believe that my two best friends would be so deceitful to me, and yet still pretend to love and care for me. I must get away from here for a while, I said to myself. I heard a knock on the door, "who is it?" I called.

"It's me Nicole," the voice said.

"Come in dear," I called. I really hated being stuck in this bed, but I since I was knocked out, I needed to make sure I was strong enough to be up and about.

"Nicole, is everything alright?" I asked her as she came in.

"Yes, I just wanted to make sure you were ok, and I don't know if you remember but I did go get the diary and it is safe," she said. I did forget that she came and told that already.

"Thank you sweetie, how are you feeling?" I asked.

"I am feeling good," she said. She seemed very different now, almost like there was a weight lifted off of her.

"I'm glad, how would you and the girls like to go on a spa weekend, just the four of us?" I asked.

"Oh, I would love to," she said filled with excitement.

"Good, I will make the arrangements," I said. "Nicole, I think I have been in bed long enough, would you like to join me in the kitchen for some breakfast and coffee?" I asked.

"I would like that, but I think I will have milk instead of coffee," she said with a little giggle.

"Of course dear, milk is very good for you. Nicole your birthday is coming up soon isn't it, how many days left?" I asked hoping to make her smile.

"Oh yes it is, it is next weekend," she said.

"Ok, maybe this weekend we will go on our spa vacation, and celebrate your birthday early," I said.

"I like that idea".

As we went in the kitchen, I heard someone in there, "I wonder who is in the kitchen?" I asked Nicole, really hoping it wasn't that Nikki girl.

"I think it is Stephan," she said as we went into the kitchen. It was Stephan, thankfully.

"Victoria what are you doing up?" he asked with a voice full of concern.

"Oh, I'm sorry Stephan, I didn't mean to worry you, but the nurse said it was fine for me to be up as long as I am not in pain," I said hoping he wouldn't see through my lie. I was never a very good liar.

"Ok, my dear, but please take it easy, you gave us all a big scare," he advised with a very loving look.

"I will, I promise," I said.

"Stephan, I am taking the girls and myself to a spa this weekend to celebrate Nicole's birthday," I said hoping he wouldn't ask too many questions. "Really, Victoria are you sure that is a good idea?" he asked.

"Yes, I am positive, it will be very relaxing, and a nice girl's weekend," I said reassuring him.

"Ok, that is a good idea, the girls will enjoy it, but are you going to ask Natasha to come as well?" he asked.

"Actually no I don't think so, she is always worrying about me, and maybe she will relax this weekend or get some stuff done herself," I said trying to sound as convincing as I possibly could.

"You are very right about that, maybe she might actually get some work done," he said.

"Ok, well I am going to make all the arrangements, and we will leave in the morning. I want to get an early start, but if you don't mind I am going to have Nick drive us," I said.

"Oh that is a wonderful idea, that way he will be there if you need anything," he said.

"Coffee," I said with excitement, when I saw Nick come in carrying a cup for me.

"Yes, Miss Victoria a cup of coffee for you," Nick said, handing me the cup.

"Thank you so much Nick, I was desperately in need of coffee this morning," I said. "Also Nick, how would you like to drive me and the girls to Providence tomorrow for a girl's spa weekend?" I asked hoping he would say yes.

"Of course ma'am, but are you sure I won't be intruding on your girls weekend?" he asked.

"Absolutely not, I was hoping you would drive us there, and then take some time for yourself, if you want to pamper yourself at the spa or go shopping. Please feel free to do anything you would like," I told him, still hoping he would say yes.

"Of course ma'am, I would be honored to do so," he said.

"Good, thank you Nick," I said as I took a sip of my coffee.

"Nicole, would you like anything?" I asked.

"No thank you Victoria," she said.

"Ok, well I am going to go and make all the arrangements. I think I might go to the store to buy all of us new robes and slippers too," I said.

"Ok, well please be careful," Stephan said.

"I will, and Nicole could you keep an eye on the girls for me?" I asked.

"Yes, of course,"

"Please make sure they clean their room, and eat all their breakfast," I said, knowing full well she would do it.

"Of course, Victoria," she said.

"Come on Snickers, let's go to the store," I said knowing that the dog would follow me anyway. As I went to get my coat, Snickers ran to the room, and came back carrying something, "what is it girl?" I asked her, as I bent down to pick up the paper. It was Luke's letter. This dog was way too smart. It was almost like she could read my mind. "Good girl Snickers, thank you," I said to her.

Now, how could I find Luke? I wondered. Oh where is my phone, its ringing, but where is it. Here it is, I said to myself as I picked up and answered. “Hello,” I said.

“Victoria, are you alone?” the voiced asked.

“Yes, who is this?” I asked.

“It’s Luke,” the voice said.

“Oh, I am going to the store, can we meet?” I asked. “Can we meet in private? I don’t want to risk Nikki or Stephan finding out?” I asked.

“Yes, I have a small café next to the department store. I have an office with a back door entrance. I am there now if you want to meet me there,” he asked.

“Perfect, I need to go to the store also, so I will meet you first, then go to the store,” I said. “

“Ok, I will unlock the door, and put a do not disturb sign on my office door. I will tell my assistant to hold all calls, and tell her I am on a conference call,” he said.

How is it possible the man who I thought was trying to kill me, is my babies’ father, and now the only person I can trust, I thought to myself. Out of all the people I have ever met, I would have never thought Natasha and Stephan would be the ones to betray me, especially Natasha, she has been my best friend since we were babies. And Stephan, I have always loved him, and him to me, how could I be so stupid? I asked myself, knowing full well how it was possible. I have always been alone, always naïve, but not anymore. I will no longer be anyone's puppet or door mat, I vowed to myself.

Luke was right; there was a back entrance to his office. I pulled up next to a tree, so my car would be somewhat hidden to the road, but still not obviously hiding. I got out and looked around to see if anyone was around. I can't believe how paranoid I have become. I am constantly looking behind me, double checking everything, and this is getting ridiculous, I thought. As I knocked on the door I began to wonder if I should trust him, maybe he and his father were also trying to get my money. Maybe this is a trap, I wondered. Now, stop it, I screamed to myself, I am not going to get anywhere by being scared of what's around the corner or who's behind the door.

"Hey" Luke said as he opened the door.

"Hi, thank you for meeting me on such short notice, but I am leaving town tomorrow morning, and I needed to see you before I left," I said.

"What? Where are you going? You can't just run away from them Victoria. Nikki will not stop looking for you until she gets what she wants," he said in a very stern voice.

"Easy, please let me explain, before you go off and accuse me of running," I said in a very stern voice, maybe a little too stern.

"I shouldn't have assumed you were running," he said in a very apologetic manner.

"I'm sorry too, I shouldn't have snapped at you," I said softly.

"It's alright, now that we have that out of the way, why don't you tell me, what your plans are for this weekend?" he said with a little laugh.

"Well, Nicole's birthday is next weekend, and I thought it would be nice to take her and the little ones to Providence and have a spa weekend," I said with a smile.

"That does sound like a wonderful idea," he said.

"I was wondering if you would like to join me, and we can discuss things, and possibly create a plan?" I asked hoping he would say yes.

"Actually, I already have to go to Providence tomorrow. I have a few meetings, with some distributors, but I would like to join you after my meetings," he said.

"Ok, maybe we can meet in the lounge at the hotel, after the girls go to bed," I asked hoping it wouldn't sound like a date.

"That's a wonderful idea, I would love to see the girls, but I think it's too soon to get into that mess, I don't want to confuse them," he said.

"Thank you, you have no idea how much it means to me, that you are putting their needs and best interests first. I never questioned you as a father or anything, and I still don't but I have been raising them for years, and I love them. I hope I have always done the right thing by them," I said to him, hoping he would know how much I love them.

"I know Victoria, and for that I will always love and respect you, and I am very sorry about attacking you that morning. I never meant for you to get hurt, and I hope you believe me," he said with the deepest look of sorrow in his eyes.

"I do believe you, and I understand," I said.

"Enough of this sappy, self-pity we've gotten ourselves feeling. What hotel are you staying at?" he asked, hoping to change the subject.

"I am staying at the plaza, but I am going to tell Stephan, I am staying at a remote spa," I said.

"Ok, that's good thinking, covering your tracks, so he won't find you," he said.

"Yes, and I am using a different name, Penny Jones, it was a girl at the orphanage," I said hoping he would think I was smart, witty, or something, other than stupid.

"That is a very smart idea," he said.

"Ok, I will meet you in the lounge at 9:30, but I am really sorry, but I must be going. I need to stop and get robes and stuff for this weekend," I said as I got up to leave.

"Victoria, thank you for believing me, and I promise I will make sure they don't get a penny, or hurt you and the girls," he said. I actually believed him, but I am not going to rely on him, I will depend only on myself from now on, I thought.

"Thank you Luke and I will see you tomorrow," I said as I left.

Once I was outside, I went immediately to the store, hoping I could find what I was looking for. I looked around but I couldn't find anything that I liked, so I decided I would just buy them at the spa. As I drove home, I wondered if things would ever be normal for me and the girls. Would Nicole be ok with the baby, would she resent me for what Dominic did to her? I had so many questions about it, but how could I ask her, was she actually alright, I wondered. I have to stop worrying. I need to focus on what's at hand, and how to control the situations, but how? I asked myself. As I pulled in the driveway, I saw Sarah and Stephanie playing on the swings with Blacky. Nicole was sitting in the grass watching them, they really looked happy. It was wonderful to see the smiles, I thought.

I pulled up to the front door, so I could pack the car tonight, instead of in the morning. Nick met me at the door, like always. "Hello Nick," I said as he offered to take my coat, and get any bags out of the car. He walked out to the car before I could say not to, but he grabbed four packages out, where did those come from? I wondered to myself.

"Is there anything else Victoria?" he asked.

"No, there isn't" I said with a very puzzled look on my face.

"Is everything alright, Victoria?" Nick asked noticing the look on my face.

"Yes, umm will you take those to my room please?" I asked him, hoping he wouldn't ask any more questions.

"Of course, ma'am he said giving me a strange look.

"Thank you Nick," I said as I went out to check the girls.

They were playing so good, they didn't even notice me watching as I sat down next to Nicole. "Victoria, how was shopping?" Nicole asked.

"It was alright," I said. "Nicole, I need you to do me a favor this weekend, I am going to call in a favor to a doctor, and have him give you a full exam, and make sure everything is ok," I said to her hoping she wouldn't be mad.

"Thank you, Victoria, I know I don't deserve to have this baby or to be happy about it, but I am. I have always wanted to give someone something, and now I can give the gift of life, and I know this baby will be happy," she said.

"I am very glad you feel that way sweetie, but I am confused, why do you think you don't deserve to be happy?" I asked.

"Well, because this baby is out of wedlock, and from a married man, I have disgraced my family's name," she said. The words hit me like a hammer right in the heart. She blamed herself.

"Nicole, what happened wasn't your fault, Dominic forced himself on you," I said hoping she would understand.

"I know that Victoria, I know it wasn't my fault, but the outcome was the same," she said.

"Ok, but honey you deserve to be happy more than anyone I know, and you are going to make this baby happier than anyone could ever be," I said hoping it would make her feel better.

"Thank you Victoria," she said.

"Honey, I am going to go inside and get things together for tomorrow, so whenever you are ready to come inside, just tell them to come in," I said to her.

I was very curious what was in those packages, how could they have got into my car? I wondered. "Nick?" I called as I walked in the house.

"Yes, Miss. Victoria," Nick said as he came into the main room.

"Did you put those packages in my room?" I asked, "and is there anyone upstairs?" I asked very cautiously.

"No, ma'am Natasha and Stephan left a short while ago," he said with the strangest smile on his face.

"Thank you Nick is there something you want to tell me?" I asked skeptically.

"No ma'am," he said.

"Ok, well I am going to go and prepare for our weekend," I said still giving him a look of curiosity.

"Ok, I will get you when dinner is done," he said.

I double checked the rooms upstairs, just to make sure Nikki wasn't lurking around anywhere. She wasn't, so I figured it was safe to go and look in those packages. As I began to examine them, I listened for ticking noises, and anything else that seemed dangerous. They seemed alright, so I slowly began to unwrap the one marked with a V. As I reached the end of the wrapping, it was a plain white box, I lifted the lid off, and inside was a beautiful champagne colored satin robe, with a very elegant matching night gown, and matching slippers, they were absolutely breath taking. As I tried on the robe I noticed there was embroidery on the right just above my breast, it had V.S., I wondered what that meant. I wonder where these came from I thought as I began to open the other ones, there was a pale pink one that had Princess Stephanie on it, I couldn't help but smile when I saw that. There was one in a Lilac color that had Princess Sarah on it, it too was perfect. I opened the last one and it was a light shade of coral, and on the back it had angel wings, and on the front it said Our Angel, I knew that meant Nicole. She was truly an angel, I thought. Each nightgown was slightly different, of course Sarah and Stephanie's were cotton, and very modest, perfect for children. Nicole's was very conservative, but yet mature. As I reached in the pocket of my robe, there was a little note, I took it out, and began to read it.

Victoria, I know you looked and couldn't find anything, so I hope you don't mind, I had these made for you guys, please enjoy.

Love, Luke.

I can't believe he did that, it was very sweet, and thoughtful, I thought. "Miss. Victoria, dinner is going to be done in about an hour," Nick said from behind my door, trying to give me my privacy.

"Ok, thank you Nick, will you send Beth out to get the children?" I asked.

"Of course ma'am," he said as I heard him begin to walk away.

Then I heard another set of footsteps, but then they paused, "hello" I called out as I walked up to my door, and opened it. No one was there, "Natasha is that you?" I asked hoping I wasn't just hearing things. I really hope it's not her, she may look like Natasha but she is not Natasha, I thought to myself. I turned to go back inside my room, and I heard the footsteps again, what is that? I wondered.

"Victoria," I heard Nicole call as she came in my room.

"Yes, Nicole what is it?" I asked.

"The girls are ready for dinner, they are washed and dressed," she said smiling.

"Thank you Nicole, would you like to see the robes, you guys got for this weekend?" I asked.

"Oh yes, I would," she said.

I held up hers, "this one is yours," I said.

"Oh, it is beautiful, Victoria, I love it, thank you," she said and hugged me. These are the girls I said as I held up the other two. "Those are perfect for them," she said.

"I'm glad you like them," I said.

"Thank you Victoria," she said.

"I am very excited about this weekend, it is going to be so much fun," I told her.

"Yes, it is, why don't you see if Luke will meet us there later, and after we go to bed, you can go and meet with him? I know you two have a lot of things to discuss," Nicole said. I was in shock how did she know about Luke.

"Nicole, how did you know, Luke and I have things to discuss?" I asked.

"I'm sorry I didn't mean to pry, but I overheard you talking to him the other morning, and plan to meet, and then I heard Nick tell you he stopped by. I promise I wasn't spying, I just overheard it, but I swear I won't say a word," she said as the tears started to show in her eyes. She was always looking out for everyone, but never for herself.

"It's ok, dear I understand, but it so typical of you, to care more for everyone else than for yourself," I said as I hugged her. The girl really did have a heart as big as the ocean, if not bigger. "Let's get ready to go down to dinner," I said as we both stood up to go downstairs.

As we walked down the stairs, I noticed the way she was carrying herself. "Nicole, are you feeling alright?" I asked noticing she looked very weak, and sore.

"Yes Victoria, I am just feeling a bit tired today," she said. I could tell she was lying, but I decided for right now I would let it go, I would just keep a very close eye on her.

"Ok, honey but if you need anything please let me know," I said hoping she would.

"I will Victoria, but I am alright I promise," she said.

"Alright dear," I said knowing she really wanted to drop the discussion.

"Oh Nick, dinner looks delicious," I said as we entered the kitchen, and saw the table.

"We are having roasted duck, with a cherry wine glaze, and to compliment the main dish we are having salad, and fresh green beans drizzled with a garlic butter, and cherry wine pilaf," Nick said. I could tell he was very proud of this dinner, because he said it with such pride. Sometimes I wondered why he wasn't a chef, because I knew he was the one who helped the cook prepare the dinner.

"Thank you Nick it looks wonderful, please give the chef my compliments," I said with a smile and look, and he knew what the look meant. "Nick, where is Stephan and Natasha?" I asked just realizing they weren't joining us this evening.

"Oh, they both had meetings to attend, it seems their business partners have accidently combined a business deal, they need to go and tend to that," he said with a look of disgust on his face.

"Ok, well then Nick please get the cook, and everyone, and we can eat," I said, hoping not to sound too much like an order.

"Of course, I will be right back," he said.

"Sarah and Stephanie, how would you like to go on a spa retreat weekend tomorrow?" I asked, hoping they would be excited.

"Oh, that sounds fun, but what about Nicole?" Stephanie asked.

“Yes, dear Nicole is coming. We are going to celebrate Nicole’s birthday coming up next week,” I said hoping she would understand.

“Ok, when are we leaving?” they asked with excitement dripping off their words, and the anticipation of my answer streaming through their eyes.

“In the morning,” I said with a giggle. They are always so excited about doing different things, and going places, even if they have been there before. I could see the excitement rising in them, “ok girls but let’s keep ourselves calm, and be patient until we leave,” I advised them, knowing they were about two seconds away from jumping up and down.

“Ok, Mom we won’t, we promise,” they said with glee in their eyes.

“Victoria, may I get you anything to drink before we eat?” Nick came in and asked.

“Oh no thank you Nick,” I said. As we began to eat, I was amazed at how delicious the duck was, our cook at Dominic’s made duck before but it didn’t taste nearly as good as this. The girls even ate it, and commented on how good it was. Stephanie even had seconds, and that girl eats like a bird. I couldn’t help but wonder what Luke was having for dinner, and why he kept his father a secret, that made me a little uneasy. Why would Nick pretend not to have Luke as his son, and where was Luke's mother, was she someone who worked here before? I couldn't help getting a little consumed with questions, and doubts about Luke. I thought the two people on earth I could trust were Stephan, and Natasha but they turned out to be the ones I couldn't trust. And now I have a man who is the girls' father, and my butler's son, and who tried to kill me one morning, saying he is the only one I could trust.

"Victoria?" Nicole said taking me completely out of my own world and putting me back at the table.

"Yes, Nicole," I said trying not to sound like I wasn't paying attention.

"Is it alright if I be excused, I am feeling tired and would like to go on up to bed," Nicole asked. I could see in her eyes something wasn't right.

"Of course dear, please go on up to bed, but you might want to take a hot bath, it normally helps me relax when I am very tired," I said to her, with complete and utter worry in my eyes, and she could see it.

"Ok, I will, thank you and good night," she said as she got up to leave.

"Mom, is Nicole alright, she said earlier today she wasn't feeling well, and I noticed her clutching her stomach, like it hurt or something?" Sarah asked. I could tell she was very worried, she always was the caring one, she was far older than her years, and she picked up on people's behavior.

"Yes, honey, she is just worn out, and needs some rest, but I promise I will check on her as soon as I finish my dinner, and besides she is going to take a bath. I better let her enjoy that without being interrupted," I said hoping my calmness would let her know everything was alright. I couldn't help but worry if she is in pain she needs to tell me or let me help her.

I helped Nick clear the table, and take everything to the kitchen, after we finished eating and I sent the girls upstairs to quietly get ready for bed with Beth. "Nick, who is Luke's mother?" I asked hoping he wouldn't think I was being too personal.

"Well, Victoria I knew we were going to have this conversation sooner or later, please have a seat and a glass of wine, while I tell you," he said handing me a glass of white wine.

"I don't mean to intrude in your life, but I was just curious is all," I said trying to not to sound questioning of him.

"It's alright Victoria, if it's one thing I have learned living here at the Strong mansion, it's that secrets and lies will eventually come out, and will hurt the people we love the most," he said. The words seemed too broad for this conversation, I wonder if there are other secrets he's not telling me, I thought.

"You are very right Nick; secrets will come out in the end."

"I joined the military right out of school, and one night when I was out on leave, some buddies and I went out to a bar, and I met this woman Megan. She was beautiful as the morning sun glistening over the dew soaked lawn. She had long black hair down to the small of her back, brown almost chocolate colored eyes, very petite, she couldn't have weighed more than a buck ten, and about five foot, two. She was absolutely the most beautiful creature I had ever seen," he described to me. As he was describing her to me, I could see he longed for her again; each word out of his mouth was like he was speaking about an angel. "I finally got up enough courage to go up and talk to her, and we sat there at the bar making small talk. She asked me if I would like to go for a walk, and of course I jumped at the chance to be alone with her," he said. I could tell he was reliving the moments as he told them to me, I had never seen anyone go into such depth when they spoke of the past. “We walked along the beach, and then she invited me back to her house for a night cap. I accepted, but I told myself I wasn’t going to be intimate with her, I wanted this woman to be more than just a one night stand. I wanted her for life,” he said and then got a soft far away smile on his face. “We had a few drinks, and all it took was a very passionate kiss, and I couldn’t tell her no. I never wanted to tell her no, I would’ve given her the stars and moon from the sky that night if she asked for it. Well yes I did end up being intimate with her, and it was heaven. I have never met a woman that could make love so much, and feel so much,” he said but as he said it his smile started to fade. “We kept in contact, and I always came to see her on leave. She wrote me, and in one letter she wrote to tell me she was with child,” he said but he didn’t look sad about that. “I was ecstatic, I always wanted children, and with her as their mother, that was even better. I had every dream I had ever dreamed, in that little letter,” he continued to say. “It was perfect timing, I was scheduled to be released to come home for good in two months. I wrote her back and told her everything on how I was feeling, and how happy I was, and that I was coming home in two months. She was very happy, but then she told me she was eight months pregnant, and we had been together for almost a year, I asked her why she didn't tell me sooner, and she said she was afraid I would leave her or stop writing her, but she couldn't keep it secret anymore. I still had two months before I could come home. I wasn't sure what I could do for her at that moment, and I told her I would be home as soon as I could, but I promised I would do anything I could for her." As I sat there listening to him, I wondered why they didn't marry, they obviously loved each other enough. "She was happy with that, and she promised she would wait for me, and keep me updated on any news of her and the baby," he said but he had a look of sorrow deep in his eyes as he continued. "Her mother found out that I wouldn't be home when the baby was born, so she made her marry another man, and never told me until Luke came to find me, after her death. I never did see her again," Nick said and I saw the tears burning behind his eyelids.

"I am so sorry Nick, I didn't mean to make you relive anything," I said with the deepest sincere voice.

"Oh, it's alright Victoria, it was a long time ago, I have come to terms with it, but if you could excuse me," he said as he got up to leave.

"Nick, thank you," I said as he walked away. I couldn't imagine feeling the way he did, and never see that person again, how devastating I thought. Oh, I must go check on Nicole, I haven't heard anything out of her in a while, I thought.

As I walked up the stairs, I could hear someone crying, but it wasn't Sarah or Stephanie, is it Nicole I asked myself? I peeked in her room, but it wasn't her, she was sound asleep, and looked so peaceful, I thought. I peeked into Stephan's room, maybe Nikki was in there, and having a moment of morals. As I peeked my head into her room, it was empty. "I wonder who could be crying?" I asked myself. Moments later, I heard Nick come out of the bathroom, and his face looked streaked with tears, it was him. He was truly heartbroken over Megan. I felt terrible for asking him about her, but the joy in his eyes when he told me about her was something I only wished I could feel for someone. I think he was happy to take a trip back to her, even if it was really only for a brief moment.

As I began to put my nightgown on, I remembered the night Stephan accidently walked in on me, and how I loved him. I wish it could have stayed that way, but it didn't and now I needed to figure out a way to keep the girls and myself safe from him, and everyone else. Reality is not a friendly face right now, but hopefully it will be soon. I am sick and tired of being scared, and looking over my shoulder, I am going to get to the bottom of it all, I said to myself, hoping that this little pep talk would give me the strength I need to do what has to be done.

I laid there in bed, wondering what the morning light would bring, but all I could think about was Nicole, and how she seemed to be in distress. I must get her to the doctor tomorrow, I thought, she needs medical care, for herself and the baby. I tossed and turned most of the night, dreaming of mother, and how I could help her, or how she could help me. I woke to the sounds of Stephanie running into my bedroom, full of excitement about our new adventure today.

"Wake up, we got to leave soon," she yelled and crawled into bed with me, hoping to make me move a little faster. Not soon after Stephanie crawled in bed with me, Sarah came running in to see if I was awake.

"I'm up, and I am going to get dressed and head downstairs for some coffee. Why don't you guys go and get your breakfast, and I will be down in a minute," I said to them, knowing that would ease their anticipation for a few moments. I put on a very elegant, yet casual outfit. The black pants, made it look dressier than it actually was, and pale tank top, with a black cardigan sweater. I brushed my hair, and decided I would pin it up, it was going to be a long and hot drive.

I went into Nicole's room to wake her, but she was already up, and downstairs. I guess she too was very excited about this weekend, I thought. How lucky am I to have three wonderful girls. I was very excited myself about spending the weekend at the spa with them, I said to myself. I walked back into my room to grab our packages from Luke, so I wouldn't forget them. As I walked downstairs, I remembered the other day when I fell, and how mother was there. I know there is something I need to do for her, but what can I do, I needed to read her actual diary, not that one that Natasha and Stephan planted there. I can't believe how sneaky and manipulative they are.

I opened the kitchen door, and to my surprise Nikki was in there, I was very unsure and worried about her being alone with the girls, but they all seemed to be happy and enjoying their breakfast. Kelly was even joining her. I couldn't help but wonder if it was Natasha or Nikki, but I am sure once she opens her month, I will be about to tell, I thought. "Good Morning, everyone" I said as I poured a cup of coffee.

"So, Victoria I hear you and the girls are going to the spa today," Kelly said trying to sound informative.

"Yes, we are I want to celebrate Nicole's birthday this weekend," I said with a smile trying to sound natural.

"Well I hear the La' Bella' Dala' is the finest spa around, and their suites are absolutely breath taking," Kelly said.

"Yes, I have heard that too, that is why I decided we will stay right there at the spa, and have a quiet peaceful weekend," I said hoping they would believe me. "So Natasha what are your plans for this weekend?" I asked hoping to change the subject.

"Oh, I have tons of work to do, and meetings back to back tomorrow, I am hoping to start the ground breaking of the new location, and company," she said, sounding even more arrogant than before, it was definitely Nikki, not Natasha, I thought.

"Well girls, are you ready to get going?" I asked knowing full well they were.

"Yes, all we need to do is get Blacky in her cage and we are ready," Sarah said, sounding so mature.

I can't believe how much older and wiser she is than her years. "How about you Nicole, are you ready?" I asked with enthusiasm.

"Yes, I am. I am very excited," she said.

"Ok, will you three get the dogs, while I check to see if Nick is ready to go?" I asked.

"Yes we will," Stephanie said as she hopped out of the room. She always wanted to help with things, and whenever she got the chance she did it with pride and honor.

"Nick?" I called as I went to the study, knowing he was probably in there, waiting for me.

"Yes, Lady Victoria," he answered.

"Are you almost ready to get going? Check in is at 10:00am and the girls are extremely excited," I said with excitement myself

"Yes, Miss I will go get the car," he said.

"Actually Nick, I already had someone get it, so all we need to do is load the kids and dogs, and we are ready," I said practically jumping and down myself with excitement.

"Ok, Victoria," he said with a laugh. I think he too was excited, after all he was going to get a night off, to do whatever he wanted to do, I thought.

"Girls, are you ready, do we have the dogs?" I called to them.

"Yes, here they are," Sarah said.

"Where is Nicole?" I asked when I only saw the two of them.

"Oh, she said she would be right out; she had to use the rest room."

"Ok, well will you two put Blacky and Snickers in the car, and I will be out in a moment?" I asked them, knowing how excited they were, about helping and going away for the weekend.

"Yes, we will" Sarah said boastfully.

I was getting very concerned about Nicole. I know she is only about six months along, but she has shown signs of premature labor the past few days, I thought. Just as I was about to go up and check on her, she came down the stairs, "are you alright Nicole?" I asked.

"Yes, I am just a bit tired today," she said.

"Nicole, are you sure you're about six months?" I asked her quietly.

"No, I am not sure how far I am," she said.

"Ok, then first thing we are going to do is, see a friend of mine, and get you checked, and make sure you are alright," I told her.

"Ok, thank you Victoria," she said as she hugged me. I knew it meant a lot to her, that I cared so much, but in all reality, I would be lost without her, she is always so strong, and brave.

“Let’s get going my dear, we have a very exciting weekend planned,” I said as we walked to the car.

“Are we ready Lady Victoria?” Nick asked as we got in the car.

“Yes, we are” I said full of excitement. I couldn’t help but have my excitement a little forced, I was deeply concerned about Nicole, and I didn’t want to say anything, but I have no one to talk to about it. I don’t know who I can trust right now. The girls were very good for most of the ride, so were the dogs, it was quite peaceful, until we got into Providence and all of a sudden, reality became real.

“Oh my goodness, what is wrong Nicole? Mom!” Stephanie screamed. I turned around quickly and immediately saw it.

“Nicole!” I screamed. “Nick, get us to the hospital fast,” I screamed to him.

“Yes, ma’am,” he said as he sped up and seemed to be racing through the city to find the hospital. “Ma’am where is the hospital?” he asked trying to cover the fear in his voice.

“I don’t know” I cried. “Nicole, baby talk to me, are you alright?” I cried. She wouldn’t answer she wasn’t moving. "Girls, move over please" I cried as I climbed in the back seat. They were so scared, and there wasn't anything I could do to make them better. I needed to get Nicole to the hospital. I didn't realize how bad it was until, I got next to her, there was so much blood and her skin felt very clammy, and cool.

"Ma'am we are here," Nick yelled. I could hear the fear in his voice, he too was very fond of her, and couldn't hide his fear anymore.

"Ok, go get help, quickly" I cried. I opened the car door, and told the girls to stay put, and hold onto the dogs. They did so, but they couldn't help the tears.

"Miss what happened?" a man in a white coat asked as he and another man pulled a gurney up to the door, and began to carefully pick her up and lay her on it.

"I don't know we were driving from Riverside, and next thing I knew my daughter screamed and I turned around to see and she was like that," I cried, trying really hard to keep myself together.

"Miss, I need you to try and tell us about her, her age, weight, medical history," the man asked.

"Ok," I couldn't think clearly, I just started to cry.

"Miss, please I need you to calm yourself down, she is in very bad shape anything you can do to help, we need please."

"Ok, umm, Nick please take the girls to the park or something and please I don't want them to be here for this," I cried.

"Yes, ma'am," he said grabbing the girls.

"Miss please," the doctor said in a very demanding voice.

"Yes, I am sorry, she is almost 16, approximately 120lbs, she has been in fairly good health, she is pregnant," I said.

"I need an OB over here, asap" the man yelled.

"Thank you miss, please come with us, we are going get her to surgery, and I need you to talk to the nurse and fill out papers, please miss," the man said.

"What is the problem?" A woman came up and asked.

"She is pregnant," the doctor said.

"Ok," the woman said, and began taking vital signs, of her and the baby. "We need to get her prepped, that baby needs to come out now, if either of them are going to live," the woman said.

"Ma'am, I need to ask you a few questions," a nurse came up and asked me.

"Ok," I said as I sat down in the chair.

"Now, I know this is hard, but who are her parents, and who is the father of the baby?" she asked me.

"I am her guardian, the father of the baby, was my deceased ex-husband. I found out a few days ago that she was pregnant, then she told me, he did this to her. I am so sorry, I should've known," I screamed more at myself than anyone.

"I know this is hard, but it is not your fault," the woman said.

"I was taking her to a spa this weekend for her birthday. I was going to get her prenatal care, and make sure everything was ok, because yesterday she was carrying herself like she was in pain, and my daughter told me she had been clutching her stomach. I tried to talk to her, but she is a very brave girl, and tough, she knows I have been through hell recently and she didn't want to add to it. She is always thinking of other people, before herself," I cried.

"Ok, ma'am I need you to sign some papers, and I hate to ask you this, but who is going to care for the baby, if she doesn't survive this, I know you don't want to think about this right now, but we need to know this, because otherwise the baby will become the property of the state, and an orphan," the nurse said. "I couldn't imagine losing Nicole, but I would never abandon her baby, I said to the nurse.

"You will save my baby, and her baby," I screamed at her.

"Miss, we are doing everything we can, to help but there is a chance this is her time," she said.

"I know, but save her please," I cried, in a tone so low, full of defeat.

"Please sign the papers ma'am and I promise, we will do everything we can." I signed the papers, and just sat there completely mortified, I couldn't speak, move, I didn't even notice Luke walk in and start talking to me.

"Victoria, damn it, snap out of it," he yelled at me.

"What? I am sorry," I said in a lifeless tone.

"Victoria, you have two daughters, and a newborn baby to worry about right now, now stop this insanity, you are stronger than this, we both know it," he said wrapping his arms around me. It did work, I felt stronger, and calmer. "Now, here drink this coffee, and eat this muffin, you need to be strong, and brave right now," he demanded. I ate the muffin, and sipped on the coffee, I began to feel better.

"Victoria, what is going on, how is Nicole pregnant?" Luke asked.

I began to cry, "it was Dominic, he forced himself on her one night, I never found out until a few days ago. That was part of what this trip was about, I wanted to get her an exam and on prenatal care, because she was actually very happy about the baby, she loves this baby."

"Ok, I am sorry to hear that Nicole had to go through that, but she is strong, and right now she needs you to be strong," he said.

"Ok, but what about Sarah and Stephanie," I asked.

"I asked my sister to take the girls and Nick to her house, she has two little girls as well, and they will be safe there," he said.

"Wait, how did you know I was here, and you have a sister?" I cried in confusion.

"Yes, my sister is a few years younger than me, and she lives here in Providence. She is an elementary teacher, Nick has met her before, she is my half sister. I was actually at the park with her and her daughters when I saw Nick, and the girls, so I asked him what was going on," I could tell by his voice, he didn't want me to distrust him.

"Ok, I am sorry, I didn't mean to, but I am very worried," I said.

"I know it is alright, that is why I am here, I know you lost the only two people you can trust, but if I can help I will," he said still holding me.

"Miss Victoria?" A man came out and asked.

"Yes, that is me," I said standing up, hoping for news that they would both be alright.

"I am sorry, but she lost a lot of blood, and we couldn't save her."

"The words hit me, so hard, I dropped to the ground and screamed, "no you, she can't be gone, please," I begged.

"Miss, please come with me," the man said, "I would like to talk to you in private, please," the man asked.

"Yes," Luke said as he picked me up, and carried me to the room, I couldn't move, walk or even speak.

"I am going to ask you a few questions, I am not questioning you, or accusing you, this is standard procedure," the man said.

"Ok," I managed to say. "What medications was Nicole on?" he asked.

"None that I know of," I said.

"Ok, well we found traces of a blood thinner in her system, has she had heart problems?" he asked.

"I don't know," I said.

"Ok, well I would like to do an autopsy on her, and examine her heart, because she was very young, and her heart gave up," the man said.

"Ok, please do," I said.

"Ok, now there is the matter of the baby. I understand you are her guardian, and that entitles you to be the parent of the baby as well," the man said.

"Is the baby alright?" Luke asked the doctor. I can't believe I forgot about the baby. I mean I knew she was pregnant and all, but she is very early, I thought.

"Yes, the baby," I asked.

"Well, the baby is a little premature, but so far the vitals are good, she is only about 8 weeks premature," the doctor said.

"It's a girl?" I asked still trying to keep my tears held back.

"Yes it is a girl, and she is 4bls, 6 oz, she will need medical attention, but if she continues to breathe on her own, then she will be able to come home in a few days," the doctor said as if it was good news. He was wrong, Nicole was gone nothing was good about this, how was I going to tell the girls, I thought, oh how my heart was aching, I can't imagine life without her, she was my rock I thought to myself.

"Thank you Doctor, but may I see Nicole, please? I just want to say good bye to her," I said hoping he would say yes.

"Ok, but I am letting you know her spirit has passed on, she is finally home, so remember that when you are saying good bye," the doctor said. I was somewhat shocked by his spiritualism, I thought doctors were scientists, not spiritualists, I thought.

"Thank you, once I see her, I would really like to see her baby, if that is alright?" I asked

"Yes, I think that is a wonderful idea," he said.

"Victoria, would you like me to come with you?" Luke asked as he put his hand on mine.

"Yes, if you would" I said, as I held on tightly to his hand, and we began to walk towards the room.

"Doctor, is her body in the morgue or is it still in the room?" I asked hoping it was in the room.

"Yes, her body is in the room, I was going to ask you what her beliefs were," he said as we were still walking.

"I don't think I understand," I said with a confused look on my face.

"Would she prefer to be cremated or buried?" he asked.

"If you don't mind, Victoria I know the answer to this. Nicole was very spiritual, and had very strong moral instincts, I think she would prefer to be cremated, because then her spirit is released, and she can go where she wishes. If she is buried then she will forever be bound to this area," Luke said.

"Yes, Luke you are right. Nicole would want to be free, and be able to stay with us," I said agreeing with Luke.

"Ok, then I will let them know, so after the autopsy they can, just take her there instead of to the morgue. I don't think she would like to be stuck in there for a while," the doctor said. I was very happy with his compassion for her and us.

"This is her room, please take all the time you need," the doctor said.

"Thank you," I said as we walked in. "She looks like she is sleeping," I said to Luke.

"Yeah, she does, she looks very peaceful," he commented.

"Luke, do you think someone did this to her?" I asked him, knowing that Nikki was probably the one who had been giving her blood thinners.

"Honestly, Victoria I want to say no, but after what all I have found out about that crazy woman at your house pretending to be Natasha, I would have to say I think Nikki was behind it, but I don't know why," he said.

That is what I thought too, "what would possess her to want to kill or make Nicole ill?" I asked hoping he would know.

"I don't know, but I will go to hell and back to find out why," he said with a very strange look on his face.

I knelt down next to the bed where Nicole lay, trying not to cry, but if I was ever to say good bye to someone, and let them go it would be her. I will give her that much, I said to myself. "Luke, I would like to be alone for a moment" I said, hoping he wouldn't mind.

"Of course Victoria, please take your time," he said as he knelt down and kissed my head.

"Thank you Luke" I said as he left the room.

"Oh Nicole, where do I begin?" I said to her, knowing she wouldn't answer, but I had to tell her how I felt. I don't know if you knew this, but you were my child, you were my rock, I loved you more than any mother could love a child. Even though I wasn't your mother, in my heart I was, and you did not deserve what Dominic did to you. I am so sorry he did this to you," I cried. "Nicole, I will take your baby and raise her as my own, but I will make sure she knows who her mother was, and how wonderful a person you were. I promise you, I will find out what happened and why, and if Nikki is behind this, she will pay" I said more as a vow of vengeance than a promise. "I am sorry Nicole, but you are finally home now, so please go on like you need to, but remember I will think of you every day, and you are and will be missed," I said.

"Victoria?" I heard a whisper.

I turned to see who was there and it was my mother and Nicole, "what, how, I mean," I began to stutter.

"Relax, Victoria, I am here to take her home," mother said, "but please don't spend your days on revenge, you know who has done this, so they will get their justice.

"Please just take the baby home, and care for her" Nicole interrupted and said.

"Nicole," I started to say and cry.

"No, Victoria, you will see to Nikki's justice, I know you will, but please protect yourself and the girls. You now have three young daughters to care for, please keep them safe," Nicole said. She was still trying to protect me and the girls, I thought. "Now, Victoria, you still have my diary, that will help you, and Luke, please let Luke be there and help you, he will not betray you, and he once loved your sister, but he is not in love with her anymore. He has let her go, so you must let it go as well, trust your heart baby girl, trust your gut," mother said as she and Nicole began to disappear.

I could not believe what had just happened, was that a dream or am I in a coma again? I began to ask myself. I stood up, and kissed Nicole's head, and said good bye one more time, and left the room, I could not be in there anymore. Should I tell Luke about that or not, do I just pretend it didn't happen? I asked myself. I think I will just keep this to myself for awhile I thought. As I left the room, where I would last see Nicole, I couldn't help but feel anger, and want revenge on whom or whatever caused this. But I know it wasn't the baby's fault, the child was as innocent as it comes, just as Nicole was. Part of me was somewhat excited about the baby, babies always brought joy upon the lives they touched, and hopefully I can make this child happy, and let Nicole's memory live through all of us.

"Victoria, are you alright?" Luke asked as he came up to me.

"Yeah, I am, I guess," I said trying to keep my emotions from flowing.

"Ok, it is ok, to cry, you have just lost someone very close to you," he said trying to let me know it was ok to feel what I was feeling.

"No, Luke I have just lost a child, I may not have given birth to her, but in her heart and mine I was her mother," I cried. "I have cared for that girl since she came to us, and I thought I kept her safe, and protected her, but all I did was put her through hell. I let Dominic hurt her, then I let Nikki take her away from me," I said as the tears streamed down my face, like rapid waters.

"No, Victoria you did not, you did protect her, you are at no fault in this, sometimes bad things happen to good people, and for that it is horrible, but some things can't be prevented," Luke said in a voice so demanding, I could see that this was killing him too. He wanted to be strong for me and the girls. I took a deep breath, and sighed

"I know, I just can't stand the idea of not seeing Nicole tomorrow, or the next day, or the day after that," I said still crying.

"I am sorry, I know this is hard for you too, I don't mean to take away from your grief," I said wrapping my arms around him, and holding him tight.

"I know it is alright, I have dealt with death, loss of love, and the emptiness you are feeling right now, but it will ease, but it takes time. Unfortunately for you or I, we don't have time, we must accept this now, and face it, so we can move on. We have two people out to take everything from you, and one who is out for blood, and to top it off we have an infant who is motherless. We have two beautiful little girls who are going to be heartbroken, and have to deal with death again at such a young age. So please grieve now, so we can leave it here," he said with sympathy, yet I could see the seriousness of our situation in his eyes.

"Ok, you are right, I am good, I know what to do," I said to him with a shocking level of confidence that seemed to shock him.

"Really, are you sure, if you need more time, please by all means take it," he said softly.

"No, I am good, I am very sad, and feel many things, but if there is one more thing I can still do for Nicole, it would be not feel sorrow for her, take care of her child, and the two girls she loved more than her own life," I said as one last tear fell from my eyelid.

"Ok, let's do this," he said standing up next to me.

I was very nervous about seeing the baby, but if this baby is anything like her mother than she is going to be strong, I thought. As we reached the nursery, I paused for a brief moment. "Victoria, are you ok?" Luke asked very softly, the words dripping of concern.

"Yes, I just needed a moment to wipe away all the negativity, and welcome the joy," I said with a light giggle, half smile.

"Ok," Luke said with a soft laugh as well, he knew exactly what I was talking about.

"Miss, if you would like to hold the baby, then I am going to have to ask you to put on a gown, and wash your hands first, please. It is for the safety of the immune system," the doctor said holding out a gown.

"Of course," I said with a soft, yet nervous smile. I went and scrubbed my hands, and put the gown on, and I was shocked to see Luke had done the same. "Thank you Luke," I said as we opened the nursery door.

"Which one is yours ma'am?" the nurse asked me.

"I am not sure," I said very timidly.

"Right this way," the doctor said as he directed the nurse to Nicole's baby.

"Oh, she is beautiful," I said.

"Yes, she is, she doesn't look that small," Luke said.

"She has so much hair, and it's dark just like Nicole's" I said, you could hear the joy falling with every word that came out of my mouth. I couldn't help but feel somewhat happy; the sight of that baby seemed to make things better. As I was sitting there holding the baby, I was trying to think of a good name for her, a name that Nicole would have picked, a name that meant something to her, but what could it be? I wondered to myself. "I got it," I said out loud.

"What do you got Victoria?" Luke asked kind of confused about my little outburst.

"Her name is going to be Ashley, it was Nicole's mother's name, and I remember one day when Nicole was younger, she was talking about what a great woman she was, and how strong she was," I said to him, with a smile on my face.

"I think that is a perfect name for her Victoria," Luke said standing next to me, just watching me and the baby.

My moment of joy was abruptly ended by the sound of my phone ringing. As I picked it up to answer, I handed Ashley back to the nurse. I walked out of the room, and answered my phone. It was the house, and I couldn't help but feel scared about who might be on the other end. "Hello," I answered.

"It's over, Victoria" the voice said.

"What, who is this?" I asked.

"That doesn't concern you, all you need to know is, it's over, and I win," the voice said.

"Nikki is this you?" I asked with a shocking tone of firmness. I would not let her know I was scared.

"Oh, wow, you are smarter than I thought, but it doesn't matter anymore, Stephan and Natasha have failed, so now it is my way, and you my dear are going to wish you were still with Dominic," she said as she hung up the phone. The sound of her words, put fear over me, I couldn't help but worry about the girls.

"Luke we need to get to the girls," I cried as I began to run down the hall towards the exit.

"Victoria," Luke yelled as he came running next to me.

"I need to get to my babies," I cried.

"Ok, but please walk and calm down, people are watching and you do not want to draw any more attention to yourself than you already have, we need to blend in," he said as he put his hand on mine trying to calm me.

"Ok," I said as I began to walk.

"Who was on the phone?" he asked.

"It was Nikki, she said, It's over, Stephan and Natasha have failed, so now it is her way, and I am going to wish I was still with Dominic," I said as the tears began to fall from off my cheeks.

"Ok, I will take you to my sister's, but then we are taking the girls to a summer camp, so they will be safe," he said.

"What? no, I will not leave them, especially at some camp, where they don't know anyone," I cried.

We reached the car, and once we were in the car, I asked Luke, why he said summer camp.

"I said summer camp because they will have fun, and be safe. Nikki will assume, that you have taken the girls with you to protect them, she would never assume that you have sent them away," he said.

"Oh, I guess I understand, but how and where?" I asked.

"I know the perfect place, my sister was going to send her girls there, but she couldn't afford it, but we can. We can send her girls too, so they will all know someone, and it's far away," he said. I hated the idea of sending them away, but maybe he was right, Nikki wouldn't think I sent them away, I thought. "Look, Victoria, I can't pretend to know everything, or have any idea of what to expect, but what I do know is, they don't know me. Nikki doesn't even think you have someone to help you, so we have an advantage, and I have a plan, we are both very street smart. You grew up alone, and poor, I grew up normal, but spent a lot of time traveling and on the streets for work, so if you are willing, I think we can get through this," he said as he put his hand on my leg as a sign of comfort.

"Ok, I am with you, but please don't let any of my girls get hurt," I said in a warning tone.

"I will do my best, I am going to have my sister take all of the girls even Ashley, and have the girls at camp. She will stay with her father's sisters with Ashley," he said.

As we pulled into the driveway of his sister's, I couldn't help but wonder what I was going to tell the girls about Nicole. "Luke, what am I going to tell them?" I asked in a very sad, quiet tone.

"You are going to tell them that she went with their mother. She is finally at peace and happy, and that she will always be in their hearts, just like you did when their mother died," he said with a soft tone.

"Ok," I said as I opened the door, and walked up to the house.

"Hey, we are here," Luke yelled as he opened the door.

"Mommy," the girls said as they came running, "where is Nicole?" Stephanie asked looking behind me.

"Look baby, I am very sorry, but Nicole went with your mommy. Do you remember when you were born and she didn't come home after that?" I asked her trying to make it easier.

"Yeah, kind of" she said, and Sarah interrupted, and said,

"Yeah, I know what you mean," with a little cry.

"Well girls, Nicole had a baby, and her heart couldn't handle it, so the angels took her," I said trying not to cry, as I looked into their little faces, knowing that this was breaking their hearts.

"Nicole had a baby?" Sarah asked.

"Yes, baby, but the baby needs to be at the hospital for another day or so, but she is ok," I said.

"Mommy, will I ever see Nicole again?" Stephanie asked. I couldn't help but have tears when I heard that, Nicole loved them so much, and they loved her.

"Yes, baby, but only in your dreams, but she will always be in your hearts," I said hoping that would help. I hugged them and held them for a while.

"Victoria, I don't mean to rush, but we need to get them ready," Luke said as he came up to us.

"I know," I said in a defeated tone. "Girls, I have a surprise for you, you and the other girls are going to go to a horse camp for awhile" I said in a very happy upbeat tone, trying to make them excited.

"Why?" Sarah asked, "What are we running from?" she continued.

Before I could say anything, Luke interrupted and said "you are not running baby, you are taking an adventure, and I need you to be strong for Stephanie, and help her learn to ride horses."

"That doesn't answer my question," she demanded. I have never seen this side of her, she was far more mature and wiser than I had thought.

"Sarah, Victoria and I need to take care of some business, and instead of making you two, be bored, and have no fun, we thought it would be fun for you guys to go away. You can relax, riding horses, swim, sing songs, and experience something new," Luke said to her, and I think it worked, her eyes began to soften.

"Ok, that could be fun," she said to Stephanie, trying to help her like the idea.

"Thank you," I said to her, "I promise you will love it," I said as I hugged her tightly.

"Victoria, this is Anne, my sister," Luke said as she came into the room.

“Hi, Anne thank you very much, for helping with my girls” I said as I held out my hand to her.

“It’s nice to meet you also,” she said in a very sharp tone, and a very wary eye. “Luke can I speak to you two in the kitchen please?” she asked.

“Ok,” he said as we followed her to the kitchen.

“What is going on, how could that girl have a baby? How does sending those two away, the day their sister dies, going to help anything, there is something going on, now talk,” she demanded.

Before Luke could begin, I told her, “I know this all sounds crazy, but I have a woman who is out to kill me, and I think that is how Nicole died. I can’t risk her finding my girls, they have been through so much already. I will not make them spend another day looking over their shoulder for danger.”

“Ok, but that doesn’t help me, why is this woman trying to kill you?” Anne asked.

“Honestly, I don’t know the full, story, all I know is that she is a twin to a woman I thought was my sister, and best friend. It turns out she is really the woman who is trying to take my inheritance, and possibly my life. I am sorry if this upsets you, but I have gone through hell for a while now, and I am going to be damned if I let it continue," I said in a very demanding tone.

"Ok, I am sorry, I mean no disrespect and I am sorry if I came across to do so. I am just confused, and it is because I don't understand. When this is all over, I am hoping I get the full story," she said.

"Thank you," I said with sincerity.

"What do you need me to do?" she asked as she looked at both of us.

"If you can, we want to send all the girls to the camp, and send you and the baby to stay with your dad's sister, until we can get this mess figured out," Luke said. I could tell by the look in her eyes, she didn't like it.

"I don't like it, but I will do it," she said.

"Thank you," I said to her, hoping she knew I was grateful.

"I understand that there is a lot that I don't know, and one of those being, how that young girl got pregnant, and is now dead. But I trust my brother, and if he says this is the way things need to be done, then I will do whatever it is that I can to help," Anne said looking directly at her brother.

"Thank you Anne, I promise I will make this up to you," Luke said as he hugged her.

"Anne, can you go to the hospital with us in the morning, and take the baby home with you? We will meet you there, but for your own safety, it is best if no one but us knows that you are involved. Have Nick drive you to the hospital in the morning, and I will go in and checkout Ashley. Then when I come out, I will get into my own car, and we can meet up at the train station, where you, Nick, and Ashley will board," I said to her, hoping it was a solid plan.

"Ok, but where are you two going to stay tonight?" Anne asked.

"I am not sure of that, but I do know, that I want the girls, on the first plane, boat, or train out of this city. I want Nick to escort them, but turn around to be back in the morning, please Nick?" I asked.

"Of course, I will do anything that is needed," he said smiling at me.

"Thank you so much, and promise me you will protect all of them, please" I begged, knowing he would, I just needed to hear it.

"That goes without saying," he said.

"Ok, Victoria I need you to get the girls ready, if our plan is going to work, then the timing of this needs to be perfect. Nikki hasn't gotten here yet, so we need to be in motion and have the girls out before she arrives," Luke said.

"Ok, Anne how much money are you going to need for all of this?" I asked her.

"Well, I am not sure, I have baby clothes, and a little bit of formula, but I need diapers, and stuff. I need money for the girl's tickets for camp, but I will pay you back for those," she said.

"Of course not, that is our gift to them. Here is the money for tickets, your bus fares or whatever you prefer to ride, and here is money for the baby. This is extra for anything else you may need, if you need more, just let Nick know, he will know how to get it," I told her as I hugged her and Nick. I couldn't believe this, what was going to happen? I wondered.

"Don't worry Victoria, I will protect all of us," Nick said.

"Girls, I called as I went into the play room, I need you to gather all your stuff, you need to get going," I said hoping they were at least a little happy.

"Ok, we will," Sarah said as she started putting their stuff together.

"I want you two to know, that I love you so much, and I promise when you come home from camp, things will be better," I said, as I hugged them. "Here is a cell phone, it only has limited minutes on it, so only use it to call me. My number is the only one in there, and it's a new number, but if you need to talk or just want to say hi, you can call me. I love you both so much," I said again as I hugged them some more.

"Victoria, it's time," Luke said as he came in.

"Ok, let's go girls," I said. "Nick, here is some money for them at camp. When you get there just give it to the counselor," I said handing him some money.

"Ok, I will" Nick said as he put it in his pocket.

"Are you guys ready? This is going to be so much fun," Anne said to all of the girls, hoping to boost their excitement level.

"Yeah," they said full of fake excitement.

"I am sorry girls, but I promise you will have fun," I said hoping they would believe me.

"We love you, and we promise to have fun," Sarah said as she hugged me good bye.

"I love you too," Stephanie said as she too came up and hugged me.

"Victoria, you do need to get going," Anne said.

"Yes she is right, they have to go, and so do we, so please Victoria let's get a move on," Luke said as he laid his hand on my shoulder.

"I know, but it is so hard to leave them," I said with the tears burning behind my eyelids.

"I know how hard it is to leave a child, but sometimes, it is better for them," Luke said hugging me.

"Ok, I can do this," I said to myself. "Girls, promise me you will have fun," I said as I looked into their little faces, and I knew it was the right thing to do.

"Yes, we promise" they said.

"Ok, I have to go, but you listen to Anne, alright and Nick," I warned.

"We will," Sarah said.

As I walked out of the house, I knew I was doing the right thing, but it was still really hard, "how can I be sure Nikki won't find them?" I asked Luke.

"I promise you the girls will be great, Nikki won't think that you sent them away, she will think you are keeping them close," he said. He was right, I wouldn't think I would send them away, I thought.

"Luke, where are we going?" I asked as we pulled on to the road.

“We are going to a friend’s house tonight, where we can prepare for tomorrow,” he said. “We have a big day ahead of us, we need to meet at the hospital, and then we are getting out of town,” he continued.

“Ok,” I said with a sigh.

“Victoria, I promise I will make sure everything is alright,” Luke promised.

“I know but we need to get through this fast because I don’t know how much more I can handle, before I go completely insane,” I said as I held on to his arm.

The drive to his friend’s house wasn’t far from his sister’s, and the hospital. As we pulled into the driveway, the man who came out to greet us, looked very familiar. I was having trouble placing him.

“Luke, who is that man?” I asked with a puzzled look on my face.

“Oh, that is Sully, he was a friend of your grandfather, I believe,” he said.

“Is his name John Sully?” I asked.

“Yes, how did you know?” he asked with confusion.

“I met him at the shelter, he was the man that knew my mother,” I said with a little bit of relief in my voice.

"Sully is a wonderful man, he is honest, loyal, probably one of the finest men I have ever met," he said as he put the car in park.

"Luke, what are we going to do, how can I get this over with so I can get my girls back, safely?" I asked with desperation in my voice.

"Victoria, I promise I will do everything in my power to help you get the girls home safely, but you are going to have to trust me," he said.

"Ok," I said knowing he was right.

"Come on, let's get this done," he said as he opened his door. As I opened my door, the realizations began to set in, Nicole was gone, Natasha had betrayed me, Stephan used me, and I fell for it.

"Sully, thank you so much for helping us, I promise I will repay you," Luke said as he hugged him.

"Hey, you know her grandfather helped me out from time to time, it is the least I could do for her, especially considering all she has gone through," he said. How could a man who barely knows me, want to help me so much?

"Luke, do you have a plan?" I asked hoping he would.

"Yes, we are going to go to the hospital in the morning so we can get Ashley to my sister, and then we are heading out of town," he said.

"That's it. That is your plan?" I said in shock. "How could that be a plan? I am not running anymore," I said with a demanding tone.

"No we are not running, we are going to make her come to us, but it is going to be on our terms not hers," he said.

"Ok," I said very uncertain of what he was thinking.

"Victoria, would you like to come inside and freshen up before we hit the hay?" Sully asked trying to make me feel better.

"Yes, I would. Thank you," I said as I followed him into the house.

"The restroom is right through there," he said pointing down the hall.

"Thank you," I said. As I looked in the mirror, I wondered how I had let my life spin so out of control, how could I have been so willing to believe everything, and now I am stuck in the middle of a nightmare. I lost one of my girls, and two of them are sent away to some camp, so they are safe. Now I have a premature infant in a hospital bed, whose mother died, how did I let all of this happen? I began to cry.

"Victoria, are you alright?" I heard Luke ask from the other side of the door. I dried my eyes, and wiped my face.

"Yes I will be out in one minute," I said trying to pull myself together.

"Victoria, I am coming in," he said as he opened the door.

"I am fine Luke," I said in a short snappy tone.

"Victoria, you are safe for the time being, it is alright to let it out, get it out of your system," he said as he put his arms around me to embrace me.

"Luke I am sorry, I just don't know how I let everything spin so out of control. All I wanted to do, was protect the girls from Dominic, and now I am running from everything," I cried.

"Victoria, you have been asked to do so much, more than anyone else could ever imagine, but you are going to get through it. Once this is over you are going to go back to the Strong Mansion and live the rest of your days with three beautiful girls, in a town that has waited many years to see you."

"The diary, mother's real diary, where is it?" I asked in a desperate tone.

"What are you talking about?" Luke asked.

"When I was knocked out, mother came to me, and told me where to find the real diary, it would explain everything," I said.

"Ok, so where is it?" he asked.

I paused a moment, "where are Nicole's belongings?" I asked.

"They are right over there," he said grabbing them. I opened her bag, and sure enough it was right there. As I began to read, I was shocked it didn't say anything about twins, or Natasha being my sister.

"Luke was that letter from my grandfather a lie too?" I asked.

"I think so," he said.

"Where is the letter, Natasha got from her Grandfather?" I asked.

"I don't know, but I am sure we can find out, ask her banker?" Luke said.

"Ok, let's go now," I said.

"Victoria they are closed," he said.

"We will go to his house," I said as I walked out towards the door.

"Victoria, wait for me," he said as he grabbed our bags and coats. "Sorry Sully, I think she is on a mission now, but thank you for everything," Luke called out as we were leaving.

The Final Phase

"Victoria, are you sure you want to do this?" Luke asked.

"Yes, and I know just how we are going to do it. That banker has no clue Dominic is dead, and he is terrified of him, so I will threaten him again, and make him give me her letter." As I drove, I looked over at Luke who was sitting very calmly in the passenger seat, and I couldn't help but wonder if he had been waiting for me to blow, or was he just naturally that calm. "Luke, thank you for being by my side, you are truly the only person I trust, right now," I said as I laid my hand on his leg, as a sense of compassion towards him.

"Victoria there isn't anything in this world I wouldn't do for you, you took my girls in and gave them a wonderful life, when I couldn't," he said.

"Here it is," I said as I whipped into the driveway, hoping the banker would hear me.

"Victoria, take this" Luke said as he handed me a gun. It's not loaded but there is nothing more terrifying to a man than a frightened woman with a gun. I have a loaded one on me, but I will only use it, if I have to," he said.

"Ok," I said taking the gun. It kind of scared me to be carrying a gun, but I am going to do whatever it takes to put this nightmare behind me. I paused for a brief moment and took a deep breath, this is I thought, finally some answers. "Let's do it," I said as I opened the door, and began to walk up to the house.

As I reached the door, my heart was pounding, but I knew I couldn't turn back. I knocked heavily on the door, hoping he would answer quickly. I waited for a moment before knocking again, and just as I was about to knock again, the door opened. It wasn't him, "excuse the unexpected intrusion but I need to speak to your husband, it is vital that I see him," I said in a tone describing the urgency.

"I would like to help but I can't," the woman said.

"Please miss, I need to see him," I cried.

"Look, I understand, but he is dead I can't help you."

The words hit me like a baseball bat to the head, "What? He's dead?" I asked.

"Yes, if you would like to come in and talk, I will help but I am not going to stand out on the front steps of my house, with the neighbors watching, explaining all the wrong doings that man has done," she said in a tone so resentful it was scary.

As we sat on the sofa, I could see in her eyes, the anger she felt, the resentment she had towards her husband. Her beautiful black hair was tied so tightly up in a bun, and her clothes were draped over her shapely body, like she too was dead. "Ma'am I am very sorry for your loss, and for the intrusion, but my life, as well as my children's are at stake here," I began to say.

"Look, if you want papers or legal documents I will give them to you, but don't give me some sob story about your little perfect life, and how terrible things are right now because you're broke, I've heard that already," she snapped.

"Ok look, I don't know what your problems are, but my oldest daughter just died and her infant child is two months premature. My two little one's just got sent to some summer camp miles and miles away, so forgive me for being rude, but you don't know the first thing about my so-called perfect life," I snapped back at her in a tone that scared me.

"I am sorry, I didn't know, I thought you were like that Kelly girl, who told me all about her life, and how hard it was being poor now," she said.

"Wait, did you say Kelly, did you give her anything?" I asked.

"No, she annoyed me, so I told her he burned everything before he got killed," she said.

"How did he die?" Luke interrupted.

"Some man, killed him, because of a banking deal, that he didn't keep."

"Was that man's name Dominic?" I asked with fear dripping from the word.

"Yes, why do you know him?" she asked.

"Yes, he was my husband, and I left him, then he was hunting me, trying to kill me," I said.

"Oh, I am sorry," she said. "Did he get any documents?" I asked almost afraid to know the answer.

"No, that I do know," she said.

"I don't mean to be rude, but I need a letter, from a woman named Natasha's safe box. It is vital that I get the information," I said.

"Ok, well I have all the safe boxes here, I couldn't risk the police confiscating them for evidence," she said as she got up and walked over to the chest. As she opened it, and began rifling through boxes, she picked out one, and brought it over to me, it was labeled Natasha Strong. I opened it, and there it was the letter she got on her 18th birthday. I began to read it.

Dear Victoria, and Violet,

You don't know me, but I am your Grandfather Joseph Strong, your mother has passed away, and I am very ill, and will probably be gone by the time you receive this. Violet, I am very sorry, I tricked your mother into thinking you were dead when you were born, and I sent you away to live at the orphanage, I am so sorry, but she was so young, she couldn't raise you, so I did what I thought was best. I sent your mother's lover away as well, hoping he would never see her again, but he came back, and Victoria that is how you came to be. I tried to get her to leave the young man, but she wouldn't. She ran away with him, but God took her away from me, while giving birth to you, and your father brought you back to me, but it was too hard to look at you, you looked so much like your mother. I couldn't bear it, so I sent you to be with your sister. I know I don't deserve your respect or forgiveness, but I just am not well, and I want to leave my fortunes to you two, you deserve it far more than anyone. I have kept tabs on you over the years to make sure you were taken care of. I recently found out that Victoria you had married a despicable man, Dominic Huntsmen, if he ever learns the truth of this letter, you will be dead once you sign on the dotted line. There are many people who want our money, and fortune, so with this gift comes many dangers. But there is one man you can trust, Sully. There is only one man who knows me, with that name, and he is a wonderful man, you can trust him if you ever run into trouble. My staff at the house is awaiting your return, they will keep you safe. Please go to the bank listed below and claim your inheritance, it is my last wish to you.

Love Always,

Joseph Strong.

Now how could Natasha get this, and not us, I wondered. She had to have snuck into the office, and read it, and gotten jealous, I thought. "Well this makes more sense, it is close to the letter they forged," I said.

"Ma'am, how can I thank you, is there anything I can do to help you?" I asked.

"No, just forget my name, and never speak of this, or of my late husband, he really was a good man, he just made bad decisions," she said.

"Actually dear, I don't even know you or your husband's name, all I knew was the address to the house. Natasha called him something before but I don't remember," I said.

"Good let's keep it that way," she said as she directed us to the door.

"Thank you again," I said as we left.

"Luke, there is something I don't understand, how did Natasha get the letter, and how did she put all of this together, things don't add up?" I asked.

"Well, Victoria, maybe that is something we need to ask when we hold the cards," he said.

"Your damn right, I am going to get the answers, she has been my best friend since we were little. How could she do this to me?"

"I don't think she meant to do this to you, I think it just happened," he said.

"How can you say that, she betrayed me!" I gasped.

"Yes, but also you were marrying Dominic, and she knew what would happen if he found out, maybe at first it was to protect you, and then it spun out of control," he said.

"Maybe, but still I don't know, this is all just a mess, it almost makes me wish I never left," I cried.

"Don't you ever say that again, he was a very evil man, and he was going to kill you and my girls." The words hit like glass upside my head, his girls, he was right. They were his girls, not mine. I couldn't help but feel the tears burning beneath my eyelids.

"I didn't mean it like that. I only meant, I know what you meant," I interrupted. "They are your girls, but they are mine too," I said as the tears began to flow. "Let's just get out of here," I said hoping he would just drive.

As we drove down the road, I couldn't help but wonder what was going to happen next. "Victoria, I have an idea, just go with it," Luke said as we pulled into the hospital parking lot.

"What are we doing here?" I asked.

"We are getting Ashley, and taking her to my sister. Then we are going to the Strong mansion, catch them off guard, and then we know the girls and my sister are safe," he said.

"Ok, I love it," I said.

As I went to the nurses' station, the nurses all looked at me with such sympathy. They knew I had had a rough day. "Hello, I am here to pick up Ashley," I said.

"Ok, she is doing great, and is all set to go home, it is a bit soon, but considering the circumstances, I think it would be fine for her to go home today," the nurse said. She had very kind eyes, looked only to be maybe 23 at the most.

"Thank you, you have no idea how much it means to bring the baby home. I may not be her birth mother, but I am her mother now, and I think it would make the entire adjustment for the girls easier to have her home and situated before they return," I said, hoping she agreed.

"Of course, I will get the release papers, for you to sign. Oh, and are you going to sign your name on the birth certificate?" she asked.

"I guess, should I?" I asked.

"Yes, I think it would be safer and less complicated if everyone believes you are her mother and when she is older, it is your choice to explain things," she said. She was by far a very wise girl, but I wondered how she came to be so wise?

"Ms. Victoria, here is baby Strong," an elder nurse came in carrying the baby. The sight of that beautiful baby girl, wrapped in a pink blanket, brought tears to my eyes, all I wished was for Nicole to get just one last breath so she too could feel the joy that baby has brought with her. Feel the warmth in her arms as she held her for the first time, and felt her heart beat to the rhythm of hers. The tears began to burn beneath my eyelids as I thought of how happy Nicole was to be giving the greatest gift to someone, the gift of life. She would be happy, I thought.

"Here Mommy," the nurse said as she handed me Ashley, my new infant daughter, the sound of that, brought the raging river of emotion to me. I was happy, but I was terribly sad.

"Victoria, honey it is late, we should be taking her home, and putting her to bed," Luke said. He was right, if we were going to get through this, we needed to get a move on. "Is it alright, did all the necessary forms, and documents get taken care of?" Luke asked the nurses.

"Oh yes, you are all set, you may take the baby home, and one more thing, good luck with everything, please be careful, and whatever is going on, use caution," the nurse from this morning said as we went to leave. "Oh and don't forget soy based formula, she was having a hard time with milk based formula," she called to us from down the hall.

"Oh, thank you very much, that could have made tonight much more difficult," I said with a nervous giggle, hoping she wouldn't see through it. "Luke, will you be a dear, and help me get the door," I asked as we were approaching the door, to the exit. I couldn't get out of this hospital fast enough, I was terrified they would see through the exterior face, and see the interior. As we walked out of the hospital, it was the first time I had the feeling of being in control, and feeling that everything would be alright. I just needed to get through the next few days, and it would all be over.

"Victoria, we are going to take Ashley to my sister's house, and then we will get a plan and set it into action. I am warning you we must act tonight and begin our plan, if it is going to work," Luke said as he opened the car door, so I could put the baby in, and be on our way. "I know that we need to figure out a way for grandfather's ghost to appear to them, especially Stephan, he knew grandfather, and respected him, and grandfather trusted him, and that has to be eating at him, that he betrayed you and grandfather," Luke said.

"Ok, I think I might just know how to do that, if we give Stephan a mild sedative, then make him think I am there alone, we will tell no one of your involvement," I said as I began to think of a way to get him to confess, and give up Nikki in the process. "Then you begin to move things, and find a very deep voice inside you so Stephan thinks he is being haunted by grandfather, but first cut the power to the house, all power, we will use a recorder, and then turn that into the police," I said with a shocking level of confidence. For the first time in a long time, I knew how to control my life, and get things done. "You know Luke, if it wasn't for Natasha and Stephan's betrayal, I doubt I would have learned how to think one step ahead," I said with a laugh. It's kind of ironic.

"Yes, Victoria you have definitely showed a lot of strength and bravery lately, and I couldn't be more proud of you. You have been through so much, and you still find it in your heart to trust in yourself, and me. If I were you, I wouldn't trust anyone, or be willing to listen, but you still have that genuine look in your eyes, it's almost magical," he said.

"Thank you, Luke but if you hadn't came to me, and made me see what was going on, and opened my eyes to some tough love, I don't think I would be so strong," I said to him. As I looked into his eyes at that moment, I saw something different, I saw my future, happiness, love, midnight walks, and a life. There was no sorrow in his eyes, it was only joy.

"We are here, are you ready to tell Ashley, a better tomorrow awaits our return," Luke said to me as he held my hand. "I know it is going to be hard but it has to be done. Are you ready?" he asked again.

"Yes, I am but will you take her in there, I can't say good bye to another baby today. If I do, I won't go through with it," I said to him as I held Ashley in my arms, and whispered to her, "I love you already, and I promise I will return with a life, and future for you in my home and heart, I love you baby girl, I love you. Here please just take her in fast," I asked as the tears streaked my cheeks, and fell faster than a mid April downpour.

"Victoria, I promise this will be the last time, you ever have to say good bye to a child because of fear, this will be the last time, you will fear what tomorrow has to bring," Luke said as he knelt down to kiss my cheek. His lips were so soft and gentle I knew he was telling the truth.

I watched him put baby Ashley in his sister's arms, and I knew Nicole was up in heaven watching over us tonight, and smiling because she knows I will protect her baby, even if I didn't protect her. "Nicole if you can hear me, I am so sorry for what happened to you, and I promise

I will make it right, I promise Nicole," I cried as I looked towards the Heavens, because that is the only place I would be able to see her again.

"Are you ready?" Luke asked as he got back into the car? "It is going to be alright, the only thing we have to do is end this, they have written the story, but you my dear are writing the ending," Luke said as we pulled out of the driveway.

"Luke, thank you I can't imagine going through this without you," I said as I placed my hand on his. He squeezed my hand as he held it, to show me I didn't need to be afraid, he would be there. I looked out my window, and I couldn't help but wonder why it was so dark in the sky, it looked like we were in for a mighty storm. "Luke, are we in for a storm?" I asked.

"Yeah, my sister was very worried about it, I guess they are warning everyone to find shelter, the storm is supposed to cause flash floods, high winds, possibly a black out," he said. "I think it is going to be hard to get across the bridge tonight; maybe we should get a room, and leave early in the morning, before everything opens. We can catch them when they are getting up, they will be half asleep, and sleepy eyed," he said.

"That is a really good idea, besides what good are we if we get killed trying to defy Mother Nature?" I said with a light laugh. "There is a little hotel up ahead, if you want to stay there," I asked. The thought of staying the night in a hotel with him, made me nervous. I am trying to block these feelings I am having, but I can't. I am beginning to see him in my future, and I like it, but it still scares me.

"Ok, it looks like they have a little café in it, so we can order in," he said. "I know you are probably going to say, "I'm not hungry, but you need to eat, you need to refuel your body, we have a long day or so ahead of us, and I promise you, you will wish you ate something," he said in an advising tone. "Victoria, I know you have gone through so much, but I need you to know, I am not going anywhere. I plan on sticking around," he said.

It made me feel better knowing he would be around. "I hope you do stay around; the girls are going to learn the truth, as soon as this is over, and they will need their father," I said. Hoping that I could reassure him that he was the girl's father, and I understood that.

"Thank you, that means more to me than words could ever say. I will never forgive myself for leaving them in the first place, but I was young, and thought I had lost the love of my life. I didn't know what to do, and I knew you would and could do better for them," he said. "I know it doesn't mean much, but you have done right by them. Violet would be so happy to see the girls, and you; and probably be telling me I need to follow my heart, it is ok to love again," he said as his cheek turned crimson.

He was blushing a little, and I knew why, he was feeling the same way I was, but was ashamed to say it, because he was the love of Violet's life. But he was right, she would tell him, to love again, and tell me to take good care of him. I smiled as I thought of Violet telling me to take care of her husband.

"Here if you want to check us in, I will get our bags," he said as he handed me his credit card.

"No, I will pay for the room, you have done enough for me," I said in protest.

"No, I will pay. You just get the best room they have, and ask if there are flash lights and candles in the room, in case we lose power, those clouds are getting full, and the winds are very strong," he said as the wind caught one of the bags in his hand, and nearly knocked him over.

"I will," I said as I grabbed the card and ran inside.

"Excuse me, Sir, I am looking for a room for the night," I asked the man sitting in the chair behind the desk, looking bored.

"Ok, but I only have one left, it's the honeymoon suite, king bed, hot tub, non-smoking," he said.

"Ok, how much," I asked as I looked down at Luke's card.

"It's $80.00 for the night," he said in a tone that showed his annoyance in me.

"Ok, also I will need a menu, and does the room have candles, and a flash light, just in case the power goes out?" I asked.

"Yup, it has all of it, and there's menu's in there," he said holding his hand out for the money.

"Oh, yeah of course," I said and reached in my pocket to hand him cash.

"Here's your key, the desk is closed as of now, so I hope you don't need anything, but the café does deliver, and they will help if you need anything," he said as he tossed the key at me, and got up and walked away.

"Wow, he was rude," I thought.

"I have the key, but the only one they have was the honeymoon suite, a king bed," I said in a shy tone.

"That's alright, as long as you are comfortable, it is fine with me," he said.

"Ok, there are candles and flashlights in the room, oh and menu's," I said trying to change the subject.

"Good, we should go and order some food first," he said. "I just saw a bolt of lightning strike on the other side of town," he said.

"Ok, do you want to order, and I will bring our things to the room?" I asked as I handed him some cash.

"Ok, but I am paying."

"No, you got the room, I will get dinner," I insisted.

"Ok, what would you like to eat?" he asked.

"Just a burger or something," I said.

"Ok, I will figure it out," he said with a laugh.

As I grabbed the bags, and began walking towards the door marked honeymoon suite, and reached for the door knob, I noticed the room to the left was cracked open. Oh I hope these doors lock, I thought. I put the key in and it opened right up. I couldn't believe how clean and neat this room was, I was excepting a total dump, but it wasn't, it was gorgeous. There was even a mini bar, with whiskey, and tequila, well at least it was something to calm the nerves, I thought. Well I am going to freshen up before he returns, I thought.

I went into the bathroom, to peel off all of my worries of the day. I turned the water on, and got in, it felt great; the water really seemed to help me. I can't believe everything that has happened and yet I still know things are going to work out, I know they will, they have to. If it is one thing I learned early in life, it was God will never give you more than you can handle, and whatever doesn't kill you, will make you stronger. I had to laugh at myself for believing that, because it was true, but some days I wondered how I survived Dominic.

As I stepped out of the shower, I realized I never grabbed any clothes to put on. Well, he will be gone for a few, I will just wrap up in a towel and go out there and get dressed, I said to myself. As I wrapped up in a towel, I couldn't help but remember the night Stephan walked in on me, and how much I wanted him that night. I had loved him since I was a child, how could he betray that love, how could he use me like this, or try and hurt me? I thought. Stop it, I scolded myself, I can't live in the past, I have to focus, and get through this.

I walked out of the bathroom, and to my surprise, Luke was standing there and from the look on his face he wasn't expecting me to walk out in a towel and catch him in a towel as well.

“I am sorry, I was just going to change my clothes while you were in the shower,” he said as his face turned a vibrant shade of red.

“I forgot my clothes out here and I thought you would be gone longer,” I said as my face turned redder than his.

“I am sorry but this is too funny, we are both adults it is completely natural to change your clothes, we have nothing to be ashamed of,” he said laughing. I too started to laugh, he was right why were we so embarrassed about this?

“You’re right, I am sorry. What did the café have to eat?” I asked, changing the subject.

“Oh they had a little of everything, but burgers, or anything that you would expect to find at a restaurant,” he said with a laugh. “I got us a couple of muffins, cookies, and pie,” he said with a laugh. “I also got us a couple of peanut butter and jelly sandwiches that was about all they could make,” he said still laughing.

“Thank you, I love a good PB&J,” I said with a flirtation giggle. I couldn’t help but feel sixteen again, as I stood there in only a towel.

“Victoria, I don’t mean to pry or get personal, but I have to ask how did you get that scar on the inside of your thigh?" he asked as he pointed to the scar, that Dominic left on me one night.

"It's from Dominic. He did it shortly after we married. I found out I was pregnant and I was sick, and very tired. I didn't feel like satisfying his needs the way a wife should, and he got upset and he pushed me and I fell into the crystal vase and broke the mirror. That made him madder, and when I tried to defend myself, he became even more angry, and he sort of threw me and when I fell a piece of the broken mirror went into my thigh. I lost the baby I was carrying" as I told him that the tears began to stream down my cheeks.

"If he wasn't already dead, I would kill him myself, there is no reason for any man or woman to lay a hand of violence on anyone," he said as he grabbed me and hugged me.

"Luke, it's fine, it was a long time ago," I said as the tears streaked my face even more.

"No, it's not ok; I am guessing you cannot have kids because of that, am I right?" he asked. I could see the look in his eyes; he was furious, but just wanted to hold me at the same time.

"You are right about not being able to have kids, but it is done and in the past, and I lived through it. Just like every other time, he would have one of his fits, you are right it's not ok, but guess what? It happened and I let it. I was weak, scared and alone, or so I thought, but I had enough. And realized I wasn't as weak as he or I thought, so please don't lecture me on how no man should lay a hand on me. I understand it, believe me, I understand it, I lived it," I said with my head held high, shoulders back, and stern as all get out.

"Hey, I am sorry, I wasn't implying anything like that, I just meant to say, I am sorry it happened to you," he said as he looked me dead in the eyes. He leaned a little closer in and I did as well. Our lips touched for the first time, our bodies fell to each other, we had found what we had been longing for. His hands were firm, and strong but not overpowering, it was secure, but not restricting, it was perfect.

"Wait we can't," I said as I felt my towel hit the floor, and his manhood, press between my legs. He paused, but I wanted him more, I pressed myself to him, I couldn't say no, I didn't want to, I wanted his love, his passion, I wanted our bodies to be one. He lifted me up off my feet, and laid me on the bed, ever so gently, it wasn't anything I had felt before, it was magical, enchanting almost. I softly moaned when I felt him enter me, his body was one with mine, our hearts and souls were one.

"Victoria," he moaned as his erection pulsated deep inside my walls, his movements were gentle but firm, as he thrusted into me, I felt his grip tighten as I was reaching the maximum of him, as he began exploding with passion, he pressed his lips to mine. I was exploding with passion as well, but I felt his passion as our lips stayed connected and a tremendous journey had ended. We laid there silent for moments, still holding each other; our breathing was heavy and deep. As he began to pull himself out, he kissed me so softly, running his fingers through my hair, just as gentle.

"Victoria, I know we think we shouldn't or we can't but we can, I love you, I don't know how, or why, but I do. The days I have spent with you, have filled an emptiness I have had for a long time. I have dated women, and been with a couple of women since Violet, but no one has ever made me feel the way you do," he said still on top of me, looking deep into my eyes. I knew he was telling the truth, no strings, no games; just truth is all I see in his eyes.

"I thought I would grow to love Dominic, and forget about the man who was in my heart, Stephan, but I never did. I thought once Stephan and I were together, my troubles were over, no more lonely nights, no more feeling alone, but that didn't happen. All I did was feel more alone than I ever did, because he was lies and deceit. The days I have spent with you, make me long for the next time I will see you, they make me look at the future with you in it. I have fallen in love with you, and I really tried to fight it, and stop wanting you, but I can't. I want you in my life, my future, I love you, and when I look in your eyes, all I see is truth, love, honesty, and a future," I said as I looked into his eyes, hoping he too would see what I see when I look in his eyes.

As the lights flickered on and off, and thunder shook the whole place, everything went black. I grabbed him tighter, and fear rushed through my blood. "Victoria, are you alright?" he asked pulling me closer to him.

"Yes, it just startled me is all," I said. "Maybe we should get dressed," I said realizing we were both very vulnerable at the moment.

"Yeah, that is a good idea," he said as he let go of me.

"What's the rush?" I heard a voice ask. Panic seized me, it was Nikki, but how did she find us?

"Isn't this sweet, Stephan's little princess, in bed with her sister's husband," she cackled.

"What are you doing here Nikki?" I demanded.

"I told you the game is over, my sister may be easier to predict, but I know everything. I know about Ashley, the girls at camp, and your sweet sister," she snapped. "Now, you are going to give me what I want or you won't see any of them again, believe me, if I can kill Nicole, I can kill children," she demanded.

"You are a monster. Nicole was a child, and if you touch any of my children, I will kill you with my bare hands," I said in a tone she understood.

"I warned you, I want it all. Natasha tricked you from the beginning, but got careless, and greedy, but I have lived through hell and back. I deserve it more than you, and anyone else, so where is it?"

"What is it, you are actually looking for?" I asked. "The money, the house, what?" I demanded.

"You don't know do you?" she said with a snicker.

"No I don't," I screamed.

"There is something your grandfather has that belonged to my grandfather, it has more power than anything, and your grandfather stole it from him, along with his grand champion stud, that is worth over a hundred grand. Your grandfather stole it from him, when he worked for my grandfather."

"I don't know what you are talking about."

“Nikki, whoever told you that, lied. I have known her grandfather since I was a child, and everything he had and she has, he earned,” Luke demanded.

“I don’t care, I saw it there the other day, and if it wasn’t for Stephan that moron, I would’ve had it and left, but that idiot had to go and get a conscience. That is why Nicole had to die. Stephan backed out on our deal, so I killed her,” she said in an arrogant tone.

“Look, take it if you want but leave us alone, and our children, they did nothing wrong,” Luke screamed and lunged for her voice. It was so black we couldn’t see anything, but neither could she. All I heard was a scream from her, and bang as they hit the table. “Victoria find the flash light,” Luke screamed as he wrestled with her.

I scrambled to find it, I grabbed the first drawer I felt, and there was the flash light. I flicked it on, but no light. “There’s no battery,” I cried. I heard glass shatter, and then it was silent. “Luke, are you ok?” I cried. Hoping it would be him that answered.

“Luke!” I screamed again and the light flickered and came back on. I saw them laying on the floor, and then Luke mumbled

“Yeah, I am ok, but I don’t think she is,” he said.

"Nikki, are you ok?" I asked as I looked down at her lifeless body. I looked around and then I saw Stephan standing there, his hands covered in blood.

"Stephan?" I said in a hushed tone, frightened by the sight of him. "Luke," I said in a soft cry, still staring at Stephan.

"Victoria, are you ok?" Luke asked as he looked towards Stephan.

"Yeah, are you?" I cried and rushed to his side.

"Yeah, what is he doing?" Luke asked as he got up to confront Stephan.

"I don't know, he is just standing there."

Luke grabbed a cup of water off the table, and splashed it in his face, hoping to wake him, or something. "Stephan," he screamed.

"I am sorry Victoria, I am sorry," he mumbled.

"Where is Natasha?" I cried.

"She killed her," he cried as tears streamed down his cheeks. "Victoria we lied to Nikki. We told her a story about your grandfather stealing from hers, so she wouldn't take what we had scammed from you, but when we tried to tell her the truth, she wouldn't believe it, and freaked out. Then she killed Nicole and Natasha," Stephan confessed. "Also, the girls never made it to that camp, I swiped them from the bus, so Nikki wouldn't get to them, they are with Nick, so is the baby and your sister and her kids," he said still in a shocked state.

"Victoria call the cops," Luke demanded. I grabbed my phone, and called them.

"They will be here in minutes, Stephan, how could you have done all of this?" I screamed.

"I had a lot of debt, from gambling, and I needed the money so Natasha and I came up with it. Then Nikki came into the picture, and screwed everything up," he said with his head held low. "I will tell the cops everything, and go to jail, but Victoria I really did love you, and still do, I am just sorry I didn't show it, or choose it over the money," he said defeated.

The cops came and took our story, and come to find out; Stephan had stabbed Nikki, that's what had killed her. They took him away in cuffs.

"Luke, let's go get our babies and go home," I said.

"Let's go" he said taking my hand in his.

As we drove through the storm, I knew the sun was shining in my heart. Things are going to be alright, I thought. I was right, we got the girls, took his sister and kids home. Then we went home, the girls were so happy to be back, and learn the true identity of Luke, and Ashley.

Everything was good. Every morning and night I told Nicole of her baby, and sometimes I even spoke to her and my mother in my dreams. Life was finally good, I was able to live a normal life, well somewhat normal, but there was no talk of Dominic, or anyone else in the past. I missed Natasha dearly, and Stephen. We had a memorial for Natasha, nothing was said of wrong choices or bad decisions. I wanted everyone to remember her as the woman she was, not the choices she made. I mourned her death as she was my sister, nothing else. I heard news shortly after Stephen's trial that he wasn't being charged for murder, but he would be serving time for the crimes that he, Nikki, and Natasha committed, but only for two to four years. I was happy to hear that, he has always been a good friend to me, and sometimes more than that.

www.ingramcontent.com/pod-product-compliance
Lightning Source LLC
Chambersburg PA
CBHW070854250626
47159CB00003B/1064

* 9 7 8 1 8 8 6 5 2 8 0 2 4 *